Virginia Smith

Dangerous Impostor

D0057631

Love Inspired

Recycling programs for this product may not exist in your area.

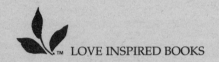 LOVE INSPIRED BOOKS

ISBN-13: 978-0-373-44476-2

DANGEROUS IMPOSTOR

www.LoveInspiredBooks.com

Printed in U.S.A.

Those who seek my life set their traps…
Come quickly to help me, O Lord my Savior.
—*Psalms* 38:12, 22

This book is dedicated to my uncle, Rick Waits.
Thank you for always being there for me.

Acknowledgments

Thanks so much to my husband, Ted,
who is my favorite research partner,
and who suffered through multiple trips to
Las Vegas to help me get the atmosphere
just right. (It's so hard being married to a
writer!) I'm grateful to Wendy Lawton, agent
extraordinaire. And thanks a HUGE amount to
my editor, Tina James, who helped me brainstorm
the idea for the Falsely Accused Support Team.
And of course I wouldn't be doing any of this
without the grace and mercy of my Lord.

ONE

A thud from the hallway outside her hotel room wrenched Lauren Bradley out of a light sleep. The ominous echo of it filled the dark room. Sleepy tendrils of a vague dream evacuated her mind in an instant, and she lay beneath the thick bedspread straining to hear past her pounding heart and the sound of the air conditioner.

A slow, muffled scraping froze the blood in her veins. That noise didn't sound like it came from the hallway. It sounded closer. Was someone in the room with her?

Don't panic. Officer Smith said it's important to stay calm.

Lessons from the self-defense class she had taken earlier this year flashed through her mind. If she was on her feet she would know exactly where to aim a crippling blow, but Officer Smith hadn't told her what to do if she was caught lying down. She drew her feet up toward her chest, preparing to defend herself against an attacker with a swift upward kick. Her ears strained to pinpoint the intruder's exact location in the unfamiliar room.

Another sound reached her ears, and this time she was easily able to locate the source. The handle of the connecting doorway to the adjoining hotel room gave a soft metallic click as someone attempted to twist the knob from the other side.

Her fear evaporated, replaced by a wave of disgust. That was no intruder inside her hotel room. That was Frank in the room next door.

Lauren threw the comforter off and swung her legs over the edge of the bed. When they'd checked into the hotel earlier, her obnoxious coworker had wagged his eyebrows when he'd seen that door.

"You know what they say, Lauren." He'd given a suggestive wink. "What happens in Vegas stays in Vegas."

Well, nothing was happening in Vegas this week. At least, nothing involving her. Even if she were to indulge in an office romance—a colossal mistake the first time, and one she did *not* intend to repeat ever again—Frank Labetti would be the last person on the face of the earth she would choose. She had barely been able to stomach sitting beside him on the plane, listening to his arrogant know-it-all chatter during the four-hour flight from Atlanta.

She stomped across the carpet in bare feet and slapped a palm against the thick wood.

"Go to sleep, Frank." Her angry shout sounded sharp in the empty room. "It's two o'clock in the morning."

No sound from the other side of the door. When she'd left Frank downstairs last night, he'd already drunk so much at dinner that his words had been starting to slur and his voice had been even louder than normal. She'd headed for the elevator, and he'd veered toward the casino. Surely he wasn't just getting back to his room. If he'd been down there drinking and gambling all night, no way he'd be up and ready to go to the conference at nine in the morning. Not that she'd mind attending conference sessions on her own—she'd prefer it, in fact—but tomorrow afternoon they had to team up and present a workshop on test tools for real-time IP networks, and she couldn't do that alone. Frank might be obnoxious, but he was the technology expert in their company.

"Frank, you'd better be sober and ready to go in the morning." She loaded her voice with the threat of dire consequences if he wasn't.

A strangled moan sounded from the other side of the door. The sound tweaked a chord of concern in Lauren. Was he sick?

"Frank, are you okay?"

The only answer was a choking cough and a worrisome gurgle almost too faint to hear.

Lauren closed her eyes and rested her forehead against the door. *Great. Just what I need. He's probably given himself alcohol poisoning. Instead of going to the conference tomorrow I'm going to have to spend my first day in Las Vegas babysitting the thirty-year-old coworker I can't stand.*

Maybe she should just go back to bed, let him sleep it off and emerge when he sobered up. That was probably the wisest course of action.

Lauren started to turn away but stopped when a second cough came from the other side of the door, this one fainter. Her resolve weakened. What if he needed medical care? He might be a jerk, but she'd be a bigger one if she ignored a sick coworker.

"Frank, are you okay?"

No answer.

Hesitant, she laid a hand on the doorknob. The other door, the one on Frank's side, was probably closed and locked. She ought to call the front desk and tell them she was worried about odd noises coming from his room. But this hotel and casino was a big place. At two in the morning it would probably take a while for them to find someone to send upstairs. What if Frank was really sick and needed help now?

Resigned, she drew on a pair of sweatpants and threw her jacket over her nightgown, unlocked the door and stepped back to swing it open.

Something tumbled to the floor and landed with a thud at her feet. Frank. For the briefest of moments she thought he had passed out leaning against the door. But then she noticed the wet, sticky streaks on the inside of the wooden door and the blood that saturated his shirt.

A scream ripped from her throat.

Music invaded Brent Emerson's dream, a familiar symphonic melody that pierced through his sleep-fogged brain. His cell phone. He cracked open one eye, and red numbers from the clock swam into view. Ten minutes past five.

"Ugh."

For a moment he considered ignoring the call. The alarm would go off in another twenty minutes anyway. What could be important enough to rob him of the last few minutes of sleep?

A list of people who would call his cell phone at this uncivilized hour paraded through his mind. His sister. Mom. The nursing home where Dad lived.

Lord, no. Please keep my family safe.

He snatched the phone off the nightstand and pushed the button to answer the call.

"Hello?" Sleep made his words scratchy.

"Is this Brent Emerson?" The voice on the other

end sounded vaguely familiar. Female. Not Mom or his sister. A nurse, maybe? His pulse quickened, pumping a shot of adrenaline to his brain that chased away the last of the sleep. Had something happened to Dad?

"Yes, this is Brent Emerson. Who is this?"

"It's Lauren. Lauren Bradley. From the office?"

An image swam into focus in his mind. An attractive young business analyst, slender, mid-twenties with honey blond hair, delicate features and intriguing green eyes. He'd interviewed and hired her three, maybe four months ago, and had only seen her from a distance since. That wasn't unusual; there weren't too many reasons for the vice president of information technology to interact with an entry-level business analyst, especially in a department as large as his.

Nor could he think of a reason for a business analyst to call him at home at five in the morning.

He sat up in bed and reached for the lamp on the nightstand. "What's up, Lauren?"

"Umm, well. I—" She inhaled a shaky breath. "I'm in Las Vegas at the INTEROP conference."

Vegas? With the time difference, that meant it was ten after two there.

"You're up kind of late, aren't you?"

"Uh, well, there's a problem. I thought I should call someone from the office. I got your cell-phone number from the departmental directory."

Her voice wavered on the last word. Was she crying? Light flooded Brent's bedroom when he twisted the lamp's knob. Crying women always stirred up emotions in him that he'd rather not deal with.

"What's the problem, Lauren?"

"It's Frank Labetti. You…you know Frank, right?"

A sob choked off the last word. She *was* crying.

He schooled his voice into a gentle tone. "Yes, I know Frank. He's there with you at the conference?"

"Yes. I mean, no. Not anymore. He's—he's dead."

"What?" Brent was on his feet beside the bed before he realized he'd moved. "How did it happen?"

"He was—he's been—shot." She was sobbing openly now, with no attempt to control it. "I found him in his hotel room a few minutes ago."

"Have you called the police?"

"Yes. They're on their way. There's…blood, so much blood." She gave herself over to weeping.

A fierce protectiveness penetrated his shock-numbed brain. This was one of his employees, on a company business trip. His responsibility. Plus, she was a frightened young woman, all alone in a strange city.

"Lauren, listen to me." He poured strength into his voice. "You did the right thing calling me. What hotel are you staying in?"

She gulped a noisy breath. "The Hollywood Hotel and Casino, right on the Strip."

"All right. I want you to keep your phone with you. I'm going to make some calls, and then I'll call you back and let you know when I'm arriving."

"You're coming here?"

Hope flooded her voice, and something in his chest gave an odd lurch in response.

"Of course I'm coming. You don't think I'd leave you there to handle this alone, do you?"

"Th—thank you."

"I'll call you back."

He disconnected the call and immediately punched in the number for his administrative assistant's cell phone. Rose was a pro when it came to finding flights. She'd either get him on the first flight from Atlanta to

Vegas, or she'd know the right buttons to push to commandeer one of the company jets.

While the call connected, he grabbed his travel bag from the closet. A list of people he needed to contact formed in his mind. Chuck, his boss and the president of the company. The director of the public relations department. His sister, to let her know he'd be out of town for a few days. He started throwing clothes and toiletries into the bag.

Shock seemed to slow his movements. Who would have a reason to shoot Frank Labetti? It must have been someone he met up with in Vegas, someone who turned out to be bad news.

Had Lauren been with them? Had she seen anything? Brent halted in the act of placing a T-shirt in the bag, his skin suddenly clammy at the thought. A pretty young woman in Las Vegas, alone and vulnerable, might be considered an easy target. Especially if she'd seen something incriminating.

Hold on, Lauren. I'm coming as fast as I can.

TWO

"Surely you understand my questions, Ms. Bradley. That's a very odd way for a coworker to behave."

Lauren forced herself not to shrink from the piercing eyes of Detective Victor Gaines. The thinly veiled accusation in his voice pounded like an insistent fist against a locked door. His questions, repeated over and over within the past couple of hours, made it sound as though he thought she and Frank had been romantically involved.

The idea was repulsive on *so* many levels.

She sat in one of two armchairs in the corner of her hotel room facing the detective, who had claimed the executive desk chair and swiveled it around to face her. His hands, folded casually in his lap, never moved, just as his expression never changed. The calm, confident mask he wore suggested that he knew her secrets, and it was just a matter of time before she admitted them all.

Another camera flash from Frank's hotel room distracted her from the detective's face. The body had been removed a few minutes ago—thank goodness—but the room was still filled with investigators. She did her best to ignore them, though her stomach churned with revulsion at the sight of the smeared wood and bloodstained carpet. Why couldn't they close that door?

She squeezed her folded arms tighter across her chest and answered as calmly as she could. "As I said before, I thought he was choking or something. I don't think it's odd at all for me to be concerned about a coworker who might have taken ill."

"But to enter the hotel room of a man you barely know wearing your pajamas." His head shook back and forth, though his eyes never left her face. "At the least, that's inappropriate. At the most, suspicious."

A flush threatened to heat her face. In retrospect, her actions did seem inappropriate, even though she'd only been trying to help. She could almost hear her father's frequent admonition, *Think with your head, Lauren, not with your heart.* She steeled herself against a stab of regret that she hadn't heeded that advice this time.

"That's why I put on my jacket and sweatpants," she told the detective for the fifth or sixth time. "I didn't bring a bathrobe, and from the sounds I heard through the door, I thought the situation might be urgent. I thought Frank might be…" She didn't finish the sentence, appalled that her suspicion had proven true, though in a gruesome way she couldn't have imagined.

"Dying?" Gains provided, the word snapping with accusation.

"Choking."

His lips twitched in an almost-smirk. "And what were you going to do? Apply the Heimlich maneuver?"

Angry steel stiffened her spine. The man's manner was starting to wear on her already thin nerves. "As a matter of fact, I do know the Heimlich maneuver."

Something passed across his face. Admiration, maybe? Or triumph, that he'd gotten a rise out of her?

A thin smile replaced the smirk. "All right, Ms. Bradley. If you don't mind, I'd like to go over your story one more time."

"It's not a *story!*" The words exploded out of her mouth, fueled by the righteous anger buzzing in her ears. "It's the truth. I'm not romantically involved with Frank Labetti. I met him three months ago when I was hired as a business analyst at Sterling Foods in Atlanta. The two of us flew to Las Vegas yesterday to attend a technology conference, checked into the hotel and had dinner in the restaurant downstairs where he drank four double bourbons." She held Gaines's eye as she repeated the details she'd already given him. "I drank iced tea. The last time I saw him was at seven-thirty when I came upstairs to my room and he was headed toward the casino. I have *no* idea what happened to him after that, until two this morning when I opened the door and found his—his—" She swallowed against a wave of revulsion that swept over her at the memory, and then drew in a fortifying breath. "His body."

The detective's eyebrows had crept upward during her tirade. "Shouting at me won't help your situation, Ms. Bradley."

My situation?

Lauren's anger faded as quickly as it had flared, replaced by a numbing shock. What was he accusing her of? Did he really think she was somehow involved in Frank's death?

But she wasn't! Surely he could see that she wasn't capable of doing anything so horrible.

I'll call Daddy, that's what I'll do. If anyone can get me out of this, it's Daddy. He always knows what to do.

The ringing of a cell phone jangled in the awkward silence of the room. It took Lauren a minute to realize the phone was hers. She reached for it on the nightstand and glanced at the screen, aware of Gaines watching her movements with the concentration of a tiger on an unsuspecting antelope.

The number displayed on the screen sent a flood of relief through her tense muscles. Thank goodness. Someone who could help her.

She spoke to the detective as she answered the call. "Here's someone who can verify what I've been telling you. My boss is here."

Brent exited the elevator and strode across plush carpet down the hotel corridor, following the signs to room number 652. He rapped on the door. It was opened almost immediately by a uniformed Las Vegas police officer.

"Hi, I'm Brent Emerson. I'm here to see Ms. Bradley."

The young officer's head cocked almost imperceptibly as he subjected Brent to a moment of scrutiny, then he jerked a nod and stepped to one side. Brent scanned the room as he crossed the threshold. A stern-faced man in a white button-down and a generic charcoal gray tie sat at the desk near the window. Feet planted squarely on the floor in front of him, strong jaw thrust forward, the man exuded the confidence of one who was comfortable with his position and enjoyed the authority it gave him.

Across from him, Lauren huddled in a standard-issue hotel armchair. Her arms were wrapped tightly across her middle, hands clutching her sleeves just above the elbows. The round eyes she turned toward him appeared larger than normal in her dainty face, and the way she pressed back into the chair, as though putting as much distance between herself and the stern-faced man stirred in him a desire to stand between them forming a protective barrier with his body.

Instead, he switched his overnight bag to his left hand and approached the man with his right extended. "Hello, I'm Brent Emerson, vice president of information technology for Sterling Foods."

The man rose and took his hand in a firm grip. "Detective Victor Gaines." His words were clipped through thin lips.

Brent turned and aimed a supportive smile toward Lauren. "Are you doing okay?"

At his soft tone, she unfolded the knots of her arms and rose. Tears sparkled in the eyes she turned up to his. For a moment he considered opening his arms and wrapping her in a hug. Though definitely not appropriate behavior between an employee and her superior, this was a special circumstance. She'd been through a horrendous experience and obviously needed comfort.

Before he could move, she folded her arms again and took a half step backward, her expression pinched. "Thank you for coming all this way, Mr. Emerson. I appreciate it. Especially since it appears I need a character witness."

Surprised, Brent turned toward the detective. "Why would she need a character witness?"

The ends of the man's mouth twitched upward in a cool smile. "A man has been killed. I'm simply attempting to uncover the facts. Perhaps you could verify some of them."

"Of course. I'll try."

Gaines took his seat and gestured toward Brent to be seated, as well. He set his overnight bag on the floor and lowered himself into the second armchair while Lauren returned to the other.

"Ms. Bradley states that she and the victim, Mr. Labetti, are in Las Vegas to attend a technology conference on behalf of your company."

"That's right." Rose had known about the conference when he called her to make his flight arrangements.

"And that she has only been employed by your company since July 18?"

Brent thought back. "I'd have to verify the date, but that sounds about right."

"How does Ms. Bradley get along with her coworkers?"

Out of the corner of his eye, Brent saw Lauren stiffen. He kept his head turned toward the detective as he answered.

"Fine, as far as I know. I head up a department with over a hundred employees, so I don't have a lot of day-to-day interaction with most of them. From what I've heard everyone seems to think she's good at her job."

"Do you know if she's particularly close to anyone?"

A strangled noise of denial emitted from Lauren's throat, but the detective held Brent's gaze.

Brent shook his head, trying to follow Gaines's thought process. Why would he ask about Lauren, when it was Frank who had been killed? The man's attitude bordered on insulting.

"I don't know the answer to that, detective. Is it important?"

Lauren blurted out, "Please tell him I wasn't having an affair with Frank."

Surprised, Brent turned a disbelieving stare on her. "Excuse me?"

"He thinks Frank and I were having an affair, and

I shot him out of a fit of jealousy or something." Tears strangled her words.

"That's an interesting theory." Gaines's stare switched to Lauren, and deepened in intensity. "I haven't said anything of the kind, but it's interesting that you came up with it on your own."

She paled, eyes widening. "You—I mean, your questions all seemed to be leading up to that."

"Wait a minute." Brent held his palms up. He didn't like the direction this conversation was going in. He speared Gaines with a direct look. "I don't know what's going on here, but if you're accusing Ms. Bradley of a crime, maybe we need to contact an attorney."

If he'd hoped the magic word, *attorney,* would have a dampening effect on the detective's accusing attitude, he was disappointed. The man's smile actually deepened into the first genuine one Brent had seen since he walked in the door. It wasn't comforting.

Gaines slapped his hands on his thighs and stood. "No need for that. I think we have everything we need for now." He looked at Lauren. "How long will you be in town?"

Her gaze flew to the connecting doorway, where someone in gray overalls with the police emblem on the breast pocket was cleaning the door with a dark blue rag. "I was scheduled to stay all week, but—"

"Good." The detective cut her off. "It would be a good idea for you to keep to your planned schedule and stick around for a few days. We might have more questions."

His meaning, though unspoken, was nonetheless apparent. Brent saw it register on Lauren's face. Her mouth gaped open as she realized she was being told not to leave town, as though she really were a suspect.

The detective nodded a farewell toward Brent and left the room. He stepped through the open connecting doorway, where his voice could be heard barking a request for an update on the investigation of the crime scene.

Brent faced his stricken employee. "I'm sure you don't have anything to worry about. He's just being thorough."

She gave a shaky nod. "It's just the thought that Frank and I…" Her words trailed off, and she shuddered. "You can't imagine how repulsive that idea is to me."

What an odd thing to say about a dead coworker. Sure, Frank wasn't the most loved guy in the information-technology department. He was known for being abrasive and something of a loudmouth. But he was intelligent, one of the smartest programmers Brent had on his staff. And he wasn't a bad-looking guy, as far as Brent could judge. Surely not repulsive.

He looked more closely at Lauren. What was it about this girl that had raised Detective Gaines's suspicions? To Brent she looked like a lovely and highly vulnerable young woman who was caught in a nightmare situation over which she had no control. But as his sister was fond of telling him, he'd always had a weakness for women in distress. The knight-in-shining-armor syndrome, Emily called it. Always charging in to rescue someone, and getting wounded in the process.

Still, Lauren was an employee of Sterling Foods, and it was his job, his responsibility, to help her.

"Don't worry. Gaines might be offensive, but he seems like he's good at his job. He'll get to the bottom of this, find out who killed Frank, and it'll all work out.

In the meantime, we'll both hang around here. I haven't been to an INTEROP conference in too many years."

Hope sprang into her face. "You'll stay in Vegas with me? Thank you, Mr. Emerson. I really appreciate that."

"Please, call me Brent. You know we don't stand on ceremony around the office."

She gave a hesitant smile, and confidence flooded the grateful eyes she turned upward to lock with his. "Thank you, Brent. I feel better already."

The sound of his whispered name stirred up an odd flutter in his stomach. Oh, yeah. Emily was right. He needed to move cautiously here. Before he donned the armor and mounted the steed, he'd better make a few calls back to Atlanta and find out more about Lauren. After all, she *looked* innocent and vulnerable, but looks could be deceiving. Gaines's obvious suspicions might be based on facts Brent didn't have access to. Leave it to him to jump to the defense of Lucrezia Borgia looking for her next victim.

THREE

"But surely you've got another room."

Lauren tightened her grip on the edge of the high counter and tried to keep her voice calm, though she wanted to shout at the hotel desk clerk.

"You can't expect me to stay in that one, where..." She closed her eyes against a resurgence of the vivid image of Frank's body tumbling through the door into her hotel room. "I'll take anything you have. The penthouse, maybe. I'll gladly pay the difference between that and the conference rate for my single room. Or a broom closet with a cot, even. I don't care."

"I'm sorry, ma'am." The older woman didn't look sorry. She looked stoic as her fingers ceased their tapping on the keyboard. "With this conference, we're completely booked. We had one suite available, and that young man just took it."

Young man? The woman nodded toward a point behind Lauren. She glanced over her shoulder, where Brent stood on the other side of the hotel lobby at the entrance to the casino, his expression serious as he spoke into a cell phone. He raised a hand and gestured in the air to emphasize something he was saying. Standing there in jeans and a long-sleeved polo he did look young, and far more relaxed than he appeared in more formal clothing at the office. When she'd interviewed with him as an applicant, she had been impressed that someone as young as he held such an important position in a company the size of Sterling Foods. It had been one of the deciding factors in her taking the job. Who wouldn't want to work for a company progressive enough to recognize talent and ability rather than age when considering the placement of their top management? A good place for a young, upwardly mobile business analyst like herself.

Not that she'd had much choice when the job offer arrived. Any job was better than no job.

A familiar pair walked past Brent, and she watched his head turn as he followed their progress. She didn't blame him for staring. How often did anyone see Elvis Presley and Frank Sinatra stroll through a hotel lobby together? When the taxi had arrived yesterday she'd noticed the hotel marquis advertising the *Best Celebrity Impersonators on the Strip!* When she'd left the restaurant and headed up to her room last night, her coworker Frank had pointed out "Barbara Streisand" and "Zsa Zsa Gabor" threading their way through the casino, talking to guests.

She shuddered at the memory of Frank.

Lauren turned back to the desk clerk. She spoke in a low voice that could not be overheard. "Look, I don't know if you're aware of what happened here last night, but a man was killed in the room next to mine. Would you be able to sleep in that room?"

Apparently the hotel management had briefed the staff on the murder, because the woman didn't appear surprised. She did, however, show the first emotion Lauren had seen. Sympathy flooded her eyes.

"I don't blame you one bit, honey, but I can't give you a room we don't have." She glanced sideways before she leaned closer to Lauren and whispered, "Maybe you should consider moving to another hotel."

Which was the first thing Lauren had considered, but the conference center was attached to this hotel. Anyplace else would be inconvenient. Besides, after that nasty detective's parting comment about keeping to her planned schedule, she was almost afraid moving to another location would make him more suspicious of her. Far better to go on with her trip as planned, and not give him any reason to watch her more closely.

Could she stay in that room for a full week without seeing Frank's body every time she glanced at the connecting door? A chill crept over her as her mind latched on to a possibility she had not considered before. What if his killer returned to the scene of the crime? Just how secure was that adjoining door?

Brent approached from behind and stood at her shoulder. "So, are we all set here?"

Lauren looked up at him. She'd never noticed how tall he was, at least a good five inches taller than she was. He must stand over six feet. Of course, she'd never stood this close to him. Nor had she noticed the color of his eyes, a smoky gray flecked with amber, like the smoldering ashes of a bonfire. His broad shoulders and strong arms made her feel almost child-sized beside him.

"They don't have any more rooms available." She put on a brave smile. "Looks like I'll have to stay where I am."

"You got our last available room," the clerk told him.

"Oh, I'm sorry." His brow creased for a moment,

then cleared. "Well, no problem. I don't mind staying in your room. You can have the suite."

He pulled his card key out of his jeans pocket and extended it to Lauren.

A wave of gratitude warmed the chill that had begun to build as Lauren had braced herself to return to her room. What a nice gesture. Not only was Brent handsome and strong and successful, he was sensitive, too. Just like Daddy, and just like—

Thoughts of the ex-boyfriend she didn't even want to *think* about slapped her in the face. She was doing it again, looking for some guy to bail her out of trouble. To take care of her. What was the matter with her that she always looked for someone else to be the strong one? Obviously she really was the pampered, helpless little girl her stepmother accused her of being.

"No." She jerked her hand away from the card.

He looked startled. "Are you sure? It's completely understandable that you wouldn't want to stay in that room after what you've been through." He pushed the key toward her again.

A sense of desperate longing nearly changed her mind. It would be so much easier to just say yes. After all, Brent had flown all this way to help her. Why not let him help?

She straightened her back and stood taller. No, she was a grown woman, twenty-four years old, and more than capable of taking care of herself. She could handle this without leaning on an emotional crutch, no matter how strong and handsome that crutch might be. And besides, Brent was her boss, and she knew better than anyone what could happen to a girl who develops emotional attachments to her boss.

Besides, surely the killer wouldn't return or the

police would have mentioned that as a possibility. Right?

"Thank you, but no." She tilted her chin upward and straightened her shoulders. "I'll be fine where I am."

Brent threaded his way through the casino, following the signs to the hotel tower elevators and the conference center. The siren song of slot machines filled the air with a seductive *ching, ching, ching,* while a sea of rainbow lights lured gamblers with promises of instant wealth. A good number of them had attracted hopeful prey, even though it was just past ten o'clock in the morning Vegas time. How anyone could sit on a chair and feed money into a machine was beyond Brent's comprehension. He worked too hard for his money to throw it away a quarter at a time.

He glanced over his shoulder where Lauren trailed behind him, her briefcase slung over one shoulder and clutched close to her side. The brave set of her chin when she refused his offer to switch hotel rooms had impressed him, even as it made him wonder at the reason for such an action. Why would she voluntarily return to a room that made her uncomfortable when there was an easy alternative?

His phone call to Rose had left him with a tendril of unease. Though she had verified Lauren's date of hire in the company's human-resource system, the applicant records had been incomplete. Lauren's pre-employment references were all stellar, but included only personal contacts and a couple of former college professors. Not a single prior employer. And yet her resume indicated that she had worked for a software firm for a year prior to applying for the job at Sterling Foods. Why were there no reference checks performed to verify her employment history?

Rose hadn't seemed concerned. "If she was still employed by the software firm when she applied here, she might have asked our recruiter not to contact her current employer. That's pretty common when someone doesn't want their boss to know they're looking for a job."

"But after she was hired, wouldn't we have run some sort of check just to verify that the information she supplied on her resume was correct?" he'd asked.

"To what end? Several people here interviewed her, including you. Your own notes are in the system. You said she was intelligent, knowledgeable and capable, and you gave the green light to hire her."

Rose's explanation seemed completely logical, but Brent had still asked her to call human resources, just to make sure that had been the case.

Now, glancing back at her lovely face and that dainty but determined chin, he felt a little guilty for asking Rose to check up on her. The bullheaded detective's suspicions had influenced him, but there was not a trace of guile in those wide green eyes. This poor young woman had been through a lot, and she deserved his support, not his suspicions.

They reached the far end of the casino, where a wide bank of elevators would take him up to his room, and a long glass-enclosed corridor veered off toward the conference center.

"I'll just go upstairs and drop my bag." Brent pushed the button and then glanced upward at the floor indicator. The elevator was a floor below them, in the parking garage. "Then I'll meet up with you at the conference registration desk."

She nodded. "I guess we'll have to find whoever's in charge of the seminars to let them know we need to cancel the session Frank and I were going to present."

"Sounds like a plan."

Lauren turned to head into the glass walkway at the same moment the elevator doors swept open. A man wearing the crisp white shirt and formal black vest of a casino dealer stepped out. Brent waited until he cleared the elevator and started toward the casino, then stepped inside.

"Good mornin', Miss Bradley."

Brent jerked to a stop at the man's words. He turned to find Lauren staring at the dealer, her expression perplexed. Her head tilted as she studied the man's face through narrowed eyes.

"Glad to see you up and about this morning. I hope Mr. Labetti is feelin' okay. He was having a pretty good time at the table last night."

The elevator doors tried to close. Brent stopped them with a hand, his attention focused on the encounter. Lauren had insisted to Detective Gaines that she'd spent the evening alone.

"The table?" She shook her head slightly. "Were you our waiter in the restaurant last night?"

The man laughed. "No, the blackjack table. I was Mr. Labetti's dealer. I guess you were havin' a pretty good time yourself if you don't remember me."

Lauren's expression went politely cold. "I'm sorry. I don't know what you're talking about. You must have me confused with someone else."

"Not likely." Now the dealer's voice took on a stiff edge. "Mr. Labetti tossed me a two-hundred-dollar chip when he called it a night. I almost felt guilty takin' it, because he wasn't walkin' real straight. I doubt if he could have made it up to his room if he'd been by himself."

Her eyes went round and snapped to Brent's. He stepped forward and let the elevator door close behind him.

"You saw who Mr. Labetti left the casino with last night?" Brent asked.

The man eyed him for a second before answering. "Yeah. But it was this morning, not night. A little before two. I was supposed to get off work at one, but Mr. Labetti was tossin' around a lot of dough and suckin' down bourbon like it was orange juice, and I knew if I stuck around he'd show his appreciation. I was right."

"Who?" Lauren stepped toward the man and demanded, "Who did he leave with?"

Heavy lines creased the man's forehead for a second as he stared at Lauren. "You're kiddin', right?" His shoulders heaved with a laugh. "You. He left with you."

FOUR

For a moment, surprise snatched the breath from Lauren's throat. Beside her, Brent's eyes had gone round for one second and then narrowed as he turned toward her.

She found her voice. "That's not true!" She faced her boss. "Honest, Brent, it's not! I don't even know how to play blackjack."

A blast of laughter came from the dealer. "Well, you were doin' pretty good last night for somebody who doesn't know how to play."

"Stop saying that! It wasn't me." She stomped her foot to emphasize her words.

The man's scraggly eyebrows arched. "O—kay. Whatever you say."

Frustration hovering on the edge of panic rose in her throat. What was going on here?

"What was I wearing? I mean—" She shook her head with a jerk, confused. "What was the person with Frank wearing?"

"I dunno." The dealer shrugged a shoulder. "A dress. Blue. Something lacy around the neck."

"There!" She rounded on Brent. "I don't own a blue dress with lace at the collar, and besides, I didn't bring a single dress with me on this trip. You can check my luggage."

He hesitated a moment, deep creases in his brow as he studied her face. Thick silence filled the immediate area around them beside the elevators, broken by the musical cry of the slot machines nearby. Lauren could almost hear Brent's thoughts. He was wondering if she really had been with Frank last night. That nasty Detective Gaines's accusations were no doubt coming back to him. Brent might even think she'd shot Frank. The absence of a dress was not valid proof. Of course if she were guilty she'd be smart enough to discard the dress she'd been wearing so it wouldn't be found in her luggage. Tears blurred her vision, and she wiped them away before they could run down her cheeks. It was starting to look as if she was being framed for murder, and she had no idea why.

Brent's hand rose, and he rubbed his fingers across his mouth. "All right, everybody just stay calm." He glanced at the dealer. "Maybe the woman you saw only looked like Ms. Bradley. Is it possible you're mistaken?"

Lauren opened her mouth to protest that *of course* he was mistaken, but Brent forestalled her with a raised hand. She snapped her lips shut.

The man cocked his head and studied Lauren's face. "Y-yeah. I guess it's possible." His tone shouted the opposite. "Maybe you got a sister in town?"

Her teeth ground together, but she managed to spit out, "I'm an only child."

The awkward silence returned, but only for a moment. Then realization stole over the dealer's features, leaving a knowing smirk in its wake. His eyes slid from Brent to Lauren, and he angled his head to give her a private wink.

"Now that I think about it, I'm probably wrong." He made a show of rubbing his chin between his fingers while he studied her. "Yeah, now that I look closer, I'm sure of it. That lady last night, she was taller, I think. And her hair was lighter. Nah, it couldn't have been you after all."

Lauren was tempted to relax her rigidly held posture, but only for a second. The man was obviously lying, trying to cover for her to Brent, for some bizarre reason.

Brent wasn't buying it. He propped his hands on his hips, and his stare became hard. "Then how did you know Ms. Bradley's name?"

The dealer jerked toward him, startled by the question. Then his face cleared. "I heard her say it when she checked in. My girlfriend is a desk clerk, and I was hanging around up at the front desk, waiting for her to go on break."

"And you just happened to remember her name?"

"Hey, that's my job, to remember names. You'd be surprised how much bigger the tips are when you call a player by name." He glanced at his watch. "I gotta go. If I'm late they'll stick me in a bum location and I won't make squat in tips." He nodded a farewell at Brent and mumbled, "Sorry about the mistake," to Lauren. As he left, he once again angled his head to give her a conspiratorial wink.

When he walked away, Lauren felt slimy and slightly sick.

"It wasn't me," she told Brent, her voice choked. "Really. It must have been someone who looked like me."

The excuse sounded hollow, fake. Even she didn't

believe it, though no other explanation made sense. How could anyone look enough like her to be mistaken for her? Brent held her gaze for a long moment, and Lauren forced herself to return his without blinking. Then he gave a wordless nod and reached for the elevator button. The doors opened immediately, and he stepped inside.

"I'll see you at the conference registration desk." His tone sounded tight, guarded.

Lauren nodded. When the doors slid shut, she stood there a moment, absently examining her reflection in the shiny metal. Something was wrong, very wrong. Was someone actually trying to cast suspicion on her? Fear pressed against her chest like a weight. But why? She'd never done anything to make someone dislike her enough to frame her for murder.

Except David.

Ridiculous! That chapter of her life ended three months ago. No doubt he'd moved on by now. Besides, David had his faults, but he wouldn't get involved in anything like murder.

Lauren turned away from the elevator and adjusted her briefcase strap on her shoulder. This was all just a big mistake, and it was sure to work out in the end.

Still, as she threaded her way through the casino toward the conference center, she couldn't shake the feeling that someone was watching her, maybe even stalking her. There was, after all, a killer wandering around loose. Spooked, she glanced over her shoulder and increased her pace.

The conference director, whose name tag read Keith Long, was a slight man with pasty skin and artificially dark hair, inexpertly arranged in a sparse comb-over.

When Lauren delivered the news, his eyes bulged like a Chihuahua's.

"But you can't cancel." His nasally whine immediately set her nerves on edge. "Your workshop starts in three hours." He snatched a conference program, a glossy magazine-style booklet, off the registration table and flipped to the opening day's schedule. With a nervous finger, he stabbed at the page. "See? *The Power of Real-Time IP Networks,* presented by F. Labetti and L. Bradley of Sterling Foods. People are expecting you."

The man's voice carried in the large room. The two women seated at the registration table glanced over, then went back to helping the lines in front of them. A dozen or so conference attendees stood talking in small groups around the registration area, name badges dangling from their necks and identical canvas bags from their shoulders. Conversations halted as they turned their attention toward Lauren. Her face warmed, and she angled her back to the room and spoke quietly.

"But you don't understand." She dipped her forehead toward him and kept her voice quiet. "Frank Labetti is…no longer with us."

Irritation flickered on the man's face. "Well, if your company fired him, why didn't they send someone to take his place in this workshop? They made a commitment." His expression grew stern. "We've comped your conference fee, Ms. Bradley, in return for a presentation from Sterling Foods."

Lauren wet her dry lips. "He wasn't fired, Mr. Long. He passed away early this morning."

Long reared back, all color leaving his already pasty face. "He's dead?"

His shout silenced the room.

The buzzing in her ears *could* be anger at his insensitive bellow, or it could be a sign that she was about to faint from embarrassment. She wavered on unsteady knees and reached for the edge of the registration table.

A strong, warm hand touched the small of her back, infusing her with a steadying shot of calm. From her side, Brent smiled down at her.

"Hello. I'm Brent Emerson, VP of information technology at Sterling Foods. Is there a problem…" His gaze dropped to the name badge on the conference director's chest. "Keith, is it?"

His pleasant expression had an immediate calming effect on the director. The man's shoulders straightened, and his grip on the program booklet relaxed.

"Actually, yes, there is a problem. Ms. Bradley," he glanced at Lauren, "just informed me that her co-presenter for this afternoon's workshop is, ah, recently deceased."

A murmur of interested voices nearby buzzed. Lauren glanced around the room. Every face turned their way.

Brent followed her gaze. "Tell me, Keith, is there a place we can discuss this privately?"

"Yes, sure. Good idea."

Lauren fell in beside Brent as they followed the man down a hallway and through a door with a sign that read, "Conference Staff Only." Tables had been pushed against all four walls, their surfaces covered with computers, conference booklets, CDs and stacks of paper handouts. No one else was in the room. When the door closed behind them, the murmuring of the conference attendees ceased.

"That's better," Brent said.

He pulled out a chair and gestured for Lauren to be seated. Grateful, she sank on to the cushioned seat. She forced herself to relax against the seat back and looked expectantly up at her boss. He and Keith selected chairs of their own before Brent spoke again.

"I'm afraid Ms. Bradley is correct. Mr. Labetti was killed last night."

"Killed?" Keith shot out of the chair he'd just taken. He stood in the center of the room and turned wide eyes toward her. "I assumed you meant he'd had a heart attack or something."

Lauren shook her head and opened her mouth to provide an explanation, but Brent answered before she could.

"He was killed in this very hotel. No doubt your conference attendees will hear of it soon. Of course, people may be afraid his death is somehow related to the conference, which isn't true. We thought it would be a good idea to tell you privately, so you can decide the best way to disseminate the information with the least amount of negative impact on the conference." Brent's voice rang with cool professionalism.

Keith's shoulders rose as his chest inflated. "Yes, of course. I appreciate that. Some attendees will no doubt be alarmed. I'll have to handle this carefully." He returned to his chair.

Lauren looked down at her hands in her lap, impressed. Brent had diffused the man's panic by reminding him of his position of authority and making him feel as if he had important work to do. The truth was they had no idea why Frank had been killed, so it *could* be somehow connected to the conference, but until the police came to that conclusion, it didn't make sense to alarm anyone.

Detective Gaines didn't sound as if he thought the

*murder had anything to do with the conference. He
thinks it has something to do with* me.

Lauren's hands clasped one another at the terrible
reminder.

"In the meantime," Brent said, "obviously this afternoon's session is impossible. Perhaps you could invite
another presenter to fill the time slot. People are always
complaining about missing one great session because
they had to go to another great session conducted at the
same time. Offering a repeat of a popular topic would
probably be viewed as a benefit."

What a great idea. Lauren awarded Brent a quick
smile.

Keith's finger tapped on the arm of his chair as he
considered the idea, but then he shook his head. "We
can't do that. You have no idea how carefully we've
selected the workshops for this conference, how much
time has gone into planning the program. Real-time IP
networks are a hot topic, and this is the only practical
application session we have scheduled on the subject."
He looked at Lauren. "You'll have to do it by yourself."

Lauren jerked upright in the chair. "Me? I can't do
that. I only know the business end. This is a technical conference, and Frank is—" She stumbled over the
word. "—*Was* the technical expert."

"What about you?" Keith turned a desperate expression toward Brent. "Surely you know about your company's technology."

This guy was starting to get on her nerves. A man
was dead, for goodness' sake, and all he could think
about was his stupid conference session?

Brent opened his mouth. "That's—"

"Out of the question." Impatience made Lauren's
voice sharp. "Mr. Emerson is a vice president. He

doesn't get involved in the day-to-day technical details of the company's applications."

Brent's eyebrows arched. He spoke to Keith but kept his gaze fixed on her. "Actually, I was going to say that's not a bad idea. I make it a practice to understand the ins and outs of cutting-edge technology, especially when it's used by Sterling Foods. If Frank had any notes about what he intended to say, I think I could cover for him." He turned in the chair so his body angled toward her. "But perhaps Ms. Bradley would prefer that I conduct the session alone, which would be perfectly understandable considering all she's been through."

A flush warmed Lauren's neck. In other words, he was giving the weak, pathetic female an out. Maybe he meant the suggestion as chivalrous, but the implication that she needed to be rescued stung. Especially when that's exactly what she would prefer.

"No, of course not." She sat higher in the chair and raised her chin. "I have no problem fulfilling my obligation."

"What a relief." Keith wilted dramatically in his chair, then popped up to his feet. "I'd better get busy figuring out how to handle the news of Mr. Labetti's death. All the equipment you shipped ahead of time is in the storage room next door, clearly labeled. We kept the workshop room clear for two hours before your session begins to give you time to set up, so you should be able to get in there..." He glanced at his watch. "In about forty minutes."

He lunged forward and shook Brent's hand, nodded at Lauren and exited the room at a brisk pace.

The quiet *snick* of the door shutting echoed in Lauren's ears. Brent made no move to rise from his chair, nor did he speak. She stole a glance at him and caught him staring at her with shrewd eyes. A lump formed in her throat. What was he thinking?

"Um, thank you." She fidgeted in her chair. "For conducting the session with me, I mean. Sorry I assumed you wouldn't know the details. It's just that, well, you know." She attempted a nonchalant shrug that felt unnatural, stiff. "You're a vice president."

He stared a moment longer before the corners of his lips twitched upward in a brief smile. "I think I'm an aberration when it comes to corporate executives. I prefer crawling in the trenches with the troops to giving orders from a distance. You haven't been with the company long enough to know that."

That was completely opposite from her previous job. Sterling Foods was so much larger than the small, family-owned software company she'd gone to work for right out of college, she'd assumed the hierarchy there would be far more rigid. Shouldn't executives focus on long-term strategy and keep themselves removed from the real work? That was certainly David's approach.

An unpleasant taste assaulted her mouth at the reminder of her ex-boss, and she pushed the thought from her mind.

"So, did you and Frank work out anything?"

He *did* think she was involved with Frank. She set her tone at a subzero temperature. "Pardon me?"

"The workshop," he explained in a gentle voice. "Did you prepare a formal presentation?"

"Oh." Flustered, Lauren practically dove for her briefcase, which she'd placed on the floor beside her. "Yes. Or, actually, I did. I'm not sure what Frank planned to say. We were going to take a tag-team approach. First I'd describe the business need, then he'd take over and cover the technical details of the implementation." She extracted a copy of her presentation outline and handed it to him. "Then we were going to do a demo. That's the equipment Keith referred to. Frank shipped some computers and handheld devices ahead of time, and we were planning to set them up in the front of the room."

Pages flipped, and his eyes moved as he scanned the document. Then he shuffled them back into a semblance of order and handed them to her.

"Sounds like a plan. I can handle that. Let's go look at the equipment."

He stood and headed for the door. Lauren stuffed her presentation back into her briefcase and rose to follow him. A flutter erupted in her stomach. With all the anxiety of Frank's death and Detective Gaines's veiled insinuations, she hadn't had time to get nervous about presenting her first conference workshop. Hopefully she'd have time to go over her presentation again before the session began.

When his hand touched the knob, Brent paused. His lips pressed together, relaxed and then tightened again, as though he struggled with whether or not to say something. He finally spoke, though he didn't look at her when he did.

"When this session is over, you and I need to have a serious conversation about your previous job." He pulled the door open and left the room without looking back at her.

Lauren's mouth dried in an instant. The door slid closed behind him, but her feet refused to move.

There was only one reason he would want to talk

about Reynolds SofTech. He'd heard about her and David.

And that would certainly make him suspicious about her and Frank.

FIVE

When Brent was about to step into the storage room, his cell phone rang. He slipped it out of his pocket and glanced at the screen. Good. Mason had returned his call quickly. He spoke to Lauren as she exited the staff room.

"I need to take this. Why don't you go ahead and make sure everything we need is there?"

The nod she gave was a bit shaky. Her knuckles were white from the grip on her briefcase strap. Maybe continuing with this session wasn't such a good idea after all. He peered at her closely, trying to see the thoughts behind those lovely eyes. Was her nervousness a result of guilt? He couldn't tell.

She went into the room without a word. He tapped on his phone's screen while walking down the carpeted hallway to find a quiet corner for his conversation.

"Hey, buddy. Thanks for calling me back."

"Well, what did you expect after leaving a message like that? What are you doing in Las Vegas, and who is this 'damsel in distress who might be a killer'?"

Brent had met Mason Sinclair several years ago at the fitness center where they both worked out. Mason had just moved to Atlanta from New Mexico, where he had been a police officer, and hung out his shingle as a private investigator. They'd discovered a mutual enthusiasm for racquetball and enjoyed a friendly but highly competitive weekly game. Though they rarely discussed business, Brent guessed that maybe Mason could help him ferret out a few things.

Brent found a relatively quiet corner and leaned against the wall. "I'm out here at a technology conference."

"Oooh, sounds exciting in a geeky sort of way." Sarcasm dripped through the phone. "All I can say is, what a waste to send a religious guy like you to Vegas. You won't partake of any of the charms of Sin City. Should have taken me with you."

Brent shook his head. Mason was a great guy, but he had a sharp tongue and frequently used it to jab at Brent's faith. Sometimes it took a steel resolve not to take offense, but Brent knew that wouldn't win the guy over. Instead, he laughingly jabbed back and prayed faithfully for Mason.

"I wouldn't come within a hundred miles of this town if you were here," he responded with a laugh. Then he grew serious. "Actually, I had to fly out here unexpectedly this morning. Two of my employees came to the conference, and one of them was shot and killed last night. I think the police suspect the other one."

"Ah, the distressed damsel."

"Right. I arrived when the detective was questioning her, and it sounded like he was hammering at her pretty hard."

Mason's voice lost the sarcasm. "Describe the interrogation. What questions did he ask, and what was his tone like?"

Brent did his best to relay the details: Gaines's accusing tone, his posture, specific questions he asked and the argumentative responses to Lauren's protestations of innocence.

"Yeah, she's a suspect all right," Mason confirmed. "He was using the Reid Method of Interrogation. I've been trained in it. It's used by police all over the country when they're pretty sure the suspect is guilty. They set up an atmosphere of confrontation from the beginning and immediately turn every word into an argument. They're even taught to insult the suspect to keep the atmosphere as hostile as possible."

Brent nodded. "That's definitely what Gaines was doing."

"He was trying to wring a confession out of her. The Reid Method is extremely effective, but one of the criticisms is that it causes people to confess when they aren't really guilty." Mason paused. "So, do you think she did it?"

Brent didn't answer for a long time. What *did* he think? She certainly had opportunity and access to Frank's room. But did she have a motive? For some reason, Gaines's assertion of a relationship gone sour didn't strike him as likely. Even if the two had been romantically involved, Lauren didn't seem like the kind of person who would kill someone in a jealous rage.

On the other hand, that dealer sure sounded positive that Lauren and Frank had been at his table last night.

"I don't know," he finally said. "I don't *think* so. I'm a pretty good judge of character, and there's something about her that makes me want to believe her. But I have to say, there's enough circumstantial evidence that I can see why the cops would suspect her."

"So you think she's being framed?"

Did he? Was that dealer paid to make his accusation? Remembering the man's face as they talked, he didn't think so. And, yes, Lauren's expression had been equally truthful, equally convincing. It just didn't make sense.

"I wish I knew what I thought," he said.

"Well, here's one you can answer. Is she pretty?"

An image of Lauren swam into focus. Soft, honey-colored hair, green eyes, narrow face with full, pink lips. He swallowed. "Yeah. Really pretty."

"Uh-huh." The sarcasm returned to his friend's voice. "And you don't think that might be affecting your judgment?"

Since that question had plagued him from the time he was jolted awake this morning, Brent couldn't think of an answer.

"Tell you what." Mason sounded all business again. "Give me her name and any details you know about her past. I'll see what I can dig up."

Exactly what Brent had hoped for. "Thanks, buddy. I'll owe you for this one."

"Yeah, if I save your sorry hide from getting killed by a gorgeous black widow, you're going to owe me big-time."

A laugh huffed out of Brent's chest. "I'll buy you a hamburger when I get back to Atlanta."

"Make that a steak," Mason retorted before the line went dead.

Brent sent a quick text with the information, then pocketed his phone and headed toward the storage closet to give Lauren a hand with those computers.

Lauren wheeled a cart with boxes piled on top into the workshop room where they would conduct their session. For a moment, her breath stalled at the sight of row after row of empty chairs. There had to be a couple of hundred chairs facing a podium and a large projection screen at the far end of a huge room. Correction—*two* rooms. A collapsible wall between two smaller rooms had been opened to form a single large one. Were they expecting that many people to attend this session? Nerves flip-flopped in her stomach.

Brent let the door close behind her and grabbed the other end of the cart. "I'm not sure how Frank intended to perform the demo, but I say we set up on that long table over there—" He pointed to a conference table to one side of the podium. "—And then set the laptops across the room, on that smaller table. It'll have more of an impact if people see them physically separated."

She schooled the nerves out of her voice. "Sounds good."

Together they rolled the cart down the center aisle and rearranged the furniture. As she unloaded a pair of smaller boxes containing laptops onto the second table, her glance strayed repeatedly to the podium where she would stand during her presentation. What if she stammered or lost her place? It was one thing to look like an inept fool in front of a few computer nerds, but two hundred? *And* her boss? She dug a fingernail into the packing tape on one of the boxes and worked at prying it off while a list of things that could go wrong formed in her mind. What if she tripped and fell in the middle of the demo?

"Here, let me help."

Brent's voice at her elbow startled her, and she jumped. He gave her an odd half smile, then produced a pocket knife to slice through the tape on both boxes. Again she was struck by his powerful build, his commanding height that made her feel small and helpless.

The flutter in her stomach intensified, this time fueled by something more than nerves.

I will not allow myself to develop a crush on my boss, no matter how handsome he is.

She took a sideways step away from him. "Thank you."

"No problem." The knife blade closed with a snap and he re-pocketed it. A question formed on his brow. "I thought you said Frank shipped the equipment."

"He did."

"Then why is your name on the address label?" A strong finger tapped the box.

Lauren looked where he pointed. How weird. Why would Frank ship the equipment to her instead of himself?

"I have no idea." A sense of unease prickled at her thoughts as she tried to come up with a logical explanation. "Maybe he just packed up the boxes and let the mail-room guys handle the labeling and shipping. And maybe the guys in the mail room knew I would be here with him?" She tried to shrug, but the movement felt jerky, nervous. Too many strange things were happening today. Her brain couldn't make sense of them all and deal with a growing sense of stage fright at the same time.

Brent peered closely at her face. "Are you okay? You look kind of pale."

"I'm fine." She attempted a calm smile, but the effect was probably spoiled by her trembling chin. "Actually," she admitted, "I'm a little nervous. I haven't done many public presentations." *Like, zero.* But she saw no need to admit that to him.

"Is that all?" He blew a puff of air in a no-big-deal gesture. "Nothing to be nervous about. Just follow your notes about the business stuff, then let me take over." His fingers waved in the air like a magician. "I'll dazzle them with a bunch of important-sounding words, and they'll eat it up. Trust me—I know how to speak techno-talk. And I know this application. There's nothing they can throw at us that we can't answer."

"You, maybe." Lauren folded her arms across her middle and attempted a joke to relieve her tension. "If someone asks me anything, I just hope I don't faint from nerves."

"You won't. But if you do get nervous, you can always picture the audience in their underwear."

The image brought a hesitant smile. "I think that would make me even more nervous than before."

"Yeah, it never worked for me, either." He shrugged and placed a hand on her upper arm. "Don't worry. If you slip up, so what? It's not a disaster. I've got your back."

Warmth spread over her, resonating from his fingers. He was so close, her every breath was tinted with the masculine scent that clung to him. With an effort, she tore her gaze from his and fought against a resurgence of the flutter in her stomach.

No! I'm not doing this. It's a false feeling, an attraction to his position, not to him. I'm just feeling vulnerable right now.

What was the matter with her that she always fell for her boss? Was it the authority that guys like Brent exuded like strong cologne? Or the masculine protective instinct she sensed in him? *I've got your back.* The words sent a ripple of relief through her.

But that was wrong. She didn't need to rely on some guy to watch her back. As her new stepmother, Lisa, had told her six months ago, it was time to pull up her big-girl pants and stand on her own two feet.

She straightened her shoulders and managed a quick smile at Brent. "I'm sure I'll be fine once I get started. I'm just feeling a touch of the jitters."

"Good. Now, would you give me a hand unpacking these other boxes? It's going to take me a while to get everything connected and the network up and running."

"Sure."

Together they opened the first of two big boxes. Inside was a desktop computer and monitor, secured amid Bubble Wrap. Brent unwrapped the machine and set it in place in the center of the long table.

"There ought to be a bunch of cables in there and a couple of smaller pieces of hardware," he said as he positioned the monitor next to the system unit.

Lauren felt around the bottom of the box. "Nothing else in here. They're probably in the other box, or maybe they're in one of the laptop boxes."

She flipped open the top of the second carton and peered inside. "Yes, there's a bunch of other stuff in here."

A thick plastic bag nestled inside packing peanuts held a half dozen or so neatly wrapped cables. Two smaller pieces of equipment that looked like routers had been wrapped in Bubble Wrap and secured neatly beside another desktop computer, also wrapped in Bubble Wrap.

"Do you want me to set up the other computer?" she asked as she handed Brent the cables. "Or unpack the laptops on the other table?"

Lines appeared between his eyes. "There's another computer?"

She nodded and put her hand on the box. "It's right here."

"We only need one desktop and the two laptops. I wonder why Frank brought that one?"

"A backup, perhaps?"

His forehead cleared. "That's probably it."

He began connecting cables, and Lauren scooted the second box to the end of the table. If this was a backup, there was no need to unpack it unless Brent had trouble with the primary one. She'd just store the box in the corner until the workshop was over, then ship it back to Sterling Foods in Atlanta.

She lifted the box off the table, surprised by the unexpected weight. Nothing she couldn't handle, but this computer was a lot bigger and heavier than the other. She put the box on the floor in the corner and stood looking down into it.

"That's strange," she said.

Brent looked up from his work. "What's strange?"

She gestured toward the box. "This system is a lot older than the others. Heavier and bulkier, too. I wonder why Frank would send something this old to a technology conference? Seems like he'd want to show off the latest equipment we use."

He left his work and came to stand beside her. "Hmm. Let me take a look."

Bending at the waist, he picked up the Bubble-Wrapped computer and straightened. "It's heavy, too." He hefted the bundle in his hands, testing the weight.

Suspicion created an itchy tingle in the back of Lauren's mind. Something felt wrong about this. "Do we have time to power it up, just to see what's on it?"

The expression on Brent's face mirrored the unease she felt. "It'll only take a minute."

His knife came out of his pocket again, and he tackled the packing tape that secured the protective wrapping around the computer. When they peeled away the Bubble Wrap, Lauren saw that this was, indeed, an older-model system. Its square, boxlike shape looked like an antique next to the smaller, sleeker unit.

"Where in the world did he dig this old thing up?" Brent muttered as he wadded the wrap and tossed it into the box.

Lauren searched the bag of cables for the power cord. Nothing looked right. She checked the power outlet on the computer to make sure she was looking for the correctly shaped cable.

"There's no power cord," she told Brent. "Maybe it's in one of those smaller boxes."

She started to cross the room toward the laptops but stopped when she caught sight of the suspicion etched on Brent's face. His eyebrows lowered as he stared at the old computer.

"What?" she asked.

His head shook a tiny bit. "I don't know. But something's not right here. The weight, the balance—it's all wrong. I'm going to open it up."

At least it wasn't just her who had a bad feeling about this computer. Lauren returned to his side and watched as he once again used his pocket knife, this time as a screwdriver to loosen the screws that held the cover in place.

When he removed the last of the screws, he pocketed his knife again. With a glance at her, he said, "Now, let's see what we've got here."

When he removed the cover, Lauren couldn't hold back a gasp. Without a doubt they'd just uncovered another clue in Frank's murder, though how this piece of the puzzle fit into the whole picture, she couldn't begin to imagine.

The machine's insides had been gutted. Instead of memory boards and power supplies, the computer was stuffed with neatly bound stacks of hundred-dollar bills.

SIX

The sight of the money hit Brent like a slap on the side of his head. For a moment all he could do was stare at it. There had to be thousands of dollars stashed in this computer.

"We need to call Detective Gaines." Lauren stepped away to retrieve her briefcase and dig inside.

That's exactly what they should do, but for some reason, Brent hesitated. The memory of Gaines's accusing attitude when he questioned Lauren, combined with Mason's revelation about the Reid Method of Interrogation, made it pretty obvious the detective suspected Lauren of killing Frank. The appearance of a wad of cash in a box with Lauren's name on it would pretty much guarantee her a trip to police headquarters for more questioning.

Maybe that's what *should* happen. The circumstances were pretty convincing. But Lauren killing Frank simply didn't make sense, no matter what the circumstances indicated. And she was really shook up, as anyone would be after seeing such a gruesome sight. If Detective Gaines used the Reid Method to interrogate her again, she might end up confessing to something she hadn't done.

The trembling of her hand as she pulled a cell phone out of her briefcase was the deciding factor for him.

"I don't think we should call the police just yet."

She paused, phone in hand, and turned round eyes his way. "Why not?"

"Because he'll consider this more evidence against you. He'll take you to jail."

Her jaw slackened as the truth of his words registered. "But…but I didn't do anything wrong." Her hand waved toward the computer. "I didn't have anything to do with this."

"Do you think Gaines will believe that?"

Her throat spasmed with a swallow, while her fingers tightened on the phone. "If we don't turn the money over, that will look even more suspicious."

True. Brent chewed the inside of his lip as he considered. "I'm not suggesting we keep the money. We'll turn it over, but I don't want to do anything hasty. We need time to think about this."

Her grip on the phone loosened, but her fingers continued to stroke the screen thoughtfully. She was obviously unconvinced.

How quickly would Mason get back to him? Maybe his buddy could dig up something that would help Lauren's cause, some assurance of her innocence, or at least of her good character. Something he could give Gaines when they handed off the money. They just needed to stall for a few hours and give Mason time to work.

He glanced at his watch. "Look, we have about ninety minutes before our session begins. Let's just put the cover back on the computer and put it aside. Then when the session is over, we'll figure out the best way to handle this."

Her troubled expression turned thoughtful. "Why are you helping me this way?"

The plaintive tone of her voice stirred up protective feelings in him. Uncomfortable, he half turned toward the table and scooped up the screws he'd removed from the computer. Why *was* he helping her? Was it because she was his employee, and she was in trouble? Or maybe because he kept seeing tears sparkle in her eyes but then disappear a moment later, as though she was using all her energy to stop them, to not appear vulnerable? Or was he acting like a fool, because she was one of the most attractive women he'd ever met? Probably all of the above, but the overriding reason was just a feeling in his gut.

He held her gaze with his. "Because I believe you're innocent."

A tremble began in her lower lip, but she tightened her mouth before he could do more than notice it. She drew in a breath and blew it out. "Thank you. That means a lot to me."

Brent broke the connection of their gazes and gestured toward the computer. "Why don't you replace the cover and wrap the system back up while I set up the network for our workshop?"

With a nod, she held out her hands for the screws. When he handed them over, his fingers brushed the soft skin on the palm of her hand. The contact sent such a delicious shock up his arm he had to force himself not to jerk away. She didn't seem to notice but took the hardware and went to work.

Brent returned to the first computer. As he unwrapped the network cables, he whispered a prayer under his breath.

"Lord, let Mason find something that will help. And let him find it quick."

Lauren replaced the screws and tightened them with her fingers as best she could. She hesitated to ask Brent for his knife, because she didn't want to risk touching him again. Surely he heard her heart pound when his fingers brushed her hand.

Her stepmother was obviously right, though Lauren hated to admit it. All her life, Daddy had taken care of her. She never knew her mother, since a car accident had taken her life when Lauren was only a few months old, and he'd remained single until last year. Daddy had worked hard to ensure she didn't suffer because of only having one parent. Not only did he shower her with love, but, since he was a wealthy man, Lauren had never wanted for any need or luxury. He'd always paid all her bills, taken her on lavish vacations, bought her anything she needed or wanted. Daddy had even arranged for her first job out of college.

The computer's cover in place, she retrieved the Bubble Wrap and began folding it around the computer, all the while avoiding looking in Brent's direction. Of course, her first job had turned out to be a complete disaster, but it was her own fault, not Daddy's. Falling for David Reynolds was the stupidest thing she had ever done. He and his brother were co-owners of the private software firm where she'd worked, which meant he'd been her boss. Why had she allowed herself to get involved with him?

Because at first, I thought he shared some of Daddy's qualities. He bought me flowers and expensive per-

*fume and treated me well when we went out. And he
was strong, assertive, full of authority, like Daddy. I
didn't know he'd turn out to be* nothing *like Daddy.*

She snuck a glance at Brent, who finished hooking
up the monitor cable, pressed the power button and
dropped into a chair in front of the computer, his eyes
on the screen. Brent exhibited those same qualities. No
doubt that's what lay behind the almost magnetic pull
she felt for him.

She picked up the wrapped computer and returned
it to the box in the corner. How much money was in
there? And what in the world was Frank doing, sending it addressed to her? The more she thought about
the mail-room scenario, the less sense it made. Frank
had put her name on those boxes. Which meant he was
involved in something underhanded, probably illegal,
and had been willing to cast suspicion on her.

Well, it had worked. *Frank, if you were still alive,
I'd give you a kick in the shins.*

"This isn't going to take as long as I thought."
Brent's words sliced through her thoughts. He glanced
up at her as his fingers flew over the keyboard. "I'm
going to need one of those notebooks up and running
in a minute."

"Okay, I'll do that."

Lauren headed across the room and began unpacking the notebook boxes. She half feared she'd find another computer full of cash, but these machines both
looked to be in working order. Besides, they were so
small they wouldn't hold much anyway.

While she waited for the laptops to power up, her
gaze was drawn back to Brent across the room. During
her interview, she'd been impressed that someone his
age had attained such a high level of responsibility. Oh,

of course she'd noted his good looks, but she'd been so focused on appearing competent and qualified for the job, she hadn't felt even a stirring of attraction.

When the human resource department had called her to offer her the position, she'd been so excited. A smile curved her lips at the memory of that moment, of trying to suppress a triumphant shout when she heard the news. She'd landed this job on her own, with no help from Daddy. And it was a good job, working for a highly respected company. When she'd gone by her father's house that night to deliver the good news, even Lisa had seemed grudgingly approving. At twenty-four, Lauren was finally learning to stand on her own two feet.

And now, look at the mess she'd landed in. Her gaze slid to the box in the corner of the room, and the sense of satisfaction faded. Instead of standing, she'd just fallen headfirst into disaster, one she had no idea how to get out of on her own. Her fingernails bit into her palms as her hands clenched into fists.

It's not my fault! I didn't do anything wrong.

Somehow, she had to prove that. Because she wasn't sure her resolution to take care of herself would remain strong if Detective Gaines took her to jail in handcuffs.

SEVEN

"It works!"

Brent couldn't help return Lauren's wide smile. He sat at the main computer, and she perched on the back row of chairs on the complete opposite side of the room with a notebook in her lap. They'd gotten their network configured and connected the devices to the room's projection system. The huge screen showed a split image: half Brent's server monitoring software, and the other half the order entry form on Lauren's notebook. After their presentation, they'd be able to pass the notebooks around and allow the attendees to enter orders themselves. The screen would show the transactions updating the main database in real time. The demo Frank had designed would be impressive.

"You doubted my abilities?" Brent allowed a teasing note to creep into his voice. "I'm crushed."

Her lips twisted, though the smile didn't disappear. "Well, you *are* an executive, after all. I doubt if any of the other vice presidents could set up a server in a month, much less in under an hour."

"I told you before, I'm not a typical executive."

"That's right, you're an aberration." A low chuckle

reached his ears, a charming sound that warmed his insides. It was good to hear her laugh.

The room filled with the sound of symphonic tones, and his cell phone vibrated on the surface of the table beside the keyboard. He glanced at the screen, saw Mason's name and snatched it up.

"Hey, buddy. Have you got something for me already?" It had been just under ninety minutes since they'd talked.

"Oh, yeah. Remember that steak you owe me? It's going to be filet mignon, and it's going to cost you a bundle. And believe me, you're going to be grateful."

Despite the teasing words, the tone of Mason's voice was serious. Brent glanced up at Lauren, who was making her way to the front of the room, notebook in hand.

He stood and headed for the service door to the left of the projection screen, speaking to her as he walked. "Excuse me a minute. I need to take this."

"Sure. I'm just going to go over my presentation."

He stepped through the door into a narrow and deserted carpeted corridor, apparently used to give convention center personnel access to the conference rooms without using the main hallway. He walked toward the end, and a couple of doors away he saw a small kitchenette with an ice machine, a large coffee maker and several shelves full of pitchers, carafes, cups and glasses.

"What did you find out?" He spoke into his phone in a quiet voice.

"Just a couple of things so far, but I thought I'd better tell you. Looks like your damsel in distress really is hiding a pair of black-widow fangs."

Brent's good mood evaporated in an instant. He leaned against the wall next to the kitchen. "Tell me."

"You mentioned that there was no reference for her prior employer, so I gave Reynolds SofTech a call. I made up a fake name and told them she had applied for a job at my company, and I wanted to speak to someone who could verify her employment history there. The lady on the phone got real cautious and wouldn't tell me anything. Said she'd have to get someone to call me back. Within ten minutes, I got a call from a guy named David Reynolds, who apparently owns part of the company."

"No kidding? The owner called you back?" Brent shook his head. A company owner returning a standard employment reference call? This couldn't be good.

"Yeah. Apparently it's a fairly small company. He said Lauren Bradley worked directly for him for almost a year. When I asked if he would classify her as a good employee, he didn't even pause. Said she was deceptive and dishonest and warned me not to hire her."

"Lauren, dishonest?" He glanced down the hallway at the closed door behind which Lauren worked. It was hard to imagine her lying. Those clear green eyes were so, well, honest.

"That's what he said. She was about to get fired when she quit. Didn't even give notice, just showed up one morning, cleaned out her desk, told Reynolds she wasn't coming back and he could keep her last paycheck."

His mind worked overtime digesting this information. Walking out on a job without notice was considered highly unprofessional.

"I can't believe it," he told Mason. "She doesn't seem the type to do that. And the paycheck thing is strange, don't you think? Maybe there's more to this than meets the eye."

"Yeah, turning down money you've earned is weird, no doubt about it. That's why I did a little financial snooping. Turns out I know a guy who works for her bank, so I gave him a call and he told me something interesting."

"Isn't that illegal? How on earth did you get a bank employee to tell you anything?"

Mason dismissed that with a grunt. "Eh, he owed me. Anyway, turns out Ms. Distressed Damsel has a ton of money in her checking account. Almost sixty thousand dollars. And fifty thousand of it was just deposited last week."

The air left Brent's lungs in a rush. He sagged against the wall. "This is unbelievable. There's got to be an explanation. I can't be that wrong about her."

A heavy pause. "Uh-oh. You know what I'm hearing on this end of the conversation?"

"What?"

"I'm hearing the sounds of an unsuspecting schmuck caught in a super-sticky web. Take my advice, Brent, and don't get tangled up with this particular spider."

Sound advice. Brent recognized the wisdom, yet at the same time, he couldn't shake the feeling that Lauren was the victim.

Lord, I need some guidance, here. I'm coming up empty on ideas. What do you want me to do?

"I hear what you're saying, buddy, and I appreciate the advice." He heaved off the wall and stepped to the center of the hallway. "But could you keep poking around? There's got to be more to the story."

A resigned sigh crackled through the phone. "Okay,

but only because I want to save you from making a colossal mistake. If you get killed, I'm out a steak dinner."

Brent couldn't help but laugh. "Nice to know you care."

"One more thing, though." Mason's voice became serious. "I know a guy out there. He used to be a jailer here in Atlanta, but a couple of years ago he found Jesus and moved to Vegas to convert prostitutes or something." Brent detected an edge of sarcasm, evidence of Mason's opinion of Christians. "He's a sharp guy in spite of that, and a good man to have on your side in a fight. I'm going to text you his address and phone number as soon as we hang up. If you run into trouble, I want you to give Caleb a call."

The concern in Mason's voice touched Brent. "Thanks, buddy. I appreciate it."

He disconnected the call and headed toward the conference room. Mason was a good guy, one of only a few men Brent could call a true friend despite their differing opinions on spiritual matters. And he did trust Mason's instincts. But in this case, Mason had never met Lauren, had never seen her, hadn't heard the sincerity in her voice when she challenged that blackjack dealer. He had to be wrong about her.

As he opened the door, Brent sent a silent prayer heavenward. *Lord, please let Mason be wrong about her. And if he's not, I'd appreciate a little extra protection over the next week or so.*

Lauren's nerves calmed as she silently read through her presentation. Though she wasn't accustomed to patting her own back, she'd done a good job of outlining the business case for the network project. It flowed well and made sense. Brent's success in setting up the demo equipment had eased another nagging worry. The technology was impressive. As long as she didn't freeze when she stepped up to the podium, everything ought to go smoothly.

Then she'd be on the other side of *this* ordeal and could concentrate on digging herself out of the hole Frank had tried to bury her in.

The service door opened and Brent entered. One glimpse of his solemn expression and Lauren's cheery greeting died on her lips. Red spots blotched the skin on his neck and face. He was upset about something.

"Is everything okay?" she asked.

He didn't answer at first. His fingers held tight to his cell phone as he stared at her. No, this was more intense than a stare. He *studied* her face as though searching for something behind her eyeballs. She squirmed beneath the intensity of his examination but somehow managed to hold his gaze.

He finally broke the silence, his voice low. "We need to talk, Lauren."

Dread dropped like a weight into her stomach. He'd said earlier that they were going to talk about her job at SofTech when the presentation was over. Oh, how she'd love to avoid that conversation.

She glanced at her watch. "Our session starts in twenty minutes."

"Then I won't waste time beating around the bush." He crossed the room and slid into a chair on the front row, leaving two empties between them. "I need to know why you left your job at Reynolds SofTech."

Moisture evaporated from her mouth as the weight in her stomach doubled. A list of reasons, all of them perfectly true, paraded through her mind. The job at Sterling Foods provided more room for professional advancement. The pay was higher. The benefits were much better. But those would sound hollow in the heavy silence between them. He'd obviously heard something, so there was no sense denying anything. Time to come clean.

She lifted her chin and looked him straight in the eye. "I quit my job because I was romantically involved with my boss, and the relationship had gone sour."

Clearly, he hadn't expected that answer. His head cocked to one side, perplexed lines creasing his brow. "A relationship? You mean, like an affair?"

Heat erupted in her face. Calling it an affair made her feel cheap. She rubbed a damp palm on her slacks. "It hadn't gone that far, but not because he didn't want it to. He was—" Shame burned her cheeks. "—Applying pressure."

"Wasn't that against the company's policies?"

"No, it wasn't." The next breath came easier. She might have acted stupidly, but at least she hadn't broken any policies. "SofTech is a private, family-run business. The only human resource policies they have are ones that have developed over the years in response to legislation. They had a couple of husband-wife teams working together, and most of the Reynolds family is employed in one capacity or another."

Brent nodded slowly, his eyes narrowed. She could almost see the thoughts zipping through his brain.

"So you just decided to end the relationship, and you quit. Why didn't you give a two-week notice?"

He'd been talking with someone at SofTech. What had they told him? "I should have given a notice," she admitted. "It was unprofessional to leave as quickly as I did. I…didn't feel comfortable there anymore."

"Your former boss says you are deceptive and dishonest."

The blood in her face heated again. *David, you skunk.* Obviously, he was still holding on to a huge grudge. She had promised him when she left that she would keep her mouth shut if he would. Looks like he'd broken his part of the bargain.

She stiffened her spine. "I have never been dishonest, and the only time I was deceptive with David was during the last month of my employment, when I was looking for another job. I admit I told him I had a doctor's appointment when I went for the interview at Sterling Foods, but I couldn't tell him why for obvious reasons." She placed a hand on the empty seat cushion beside her and leaned toward Brent so he could see the truth in her eyes. "I couldn't keep working there for two reasons. First, because my relationship with David made me privileged to some…" She searched for a word. "Some questionable business practices. And second, because David was becoming possessive. He controlled every minute of my time, monitored my personal cell phone usage, even checked the mileage on my car. When I complained, he became physically rough."

Brent's lips tightened. "He hit you?"

"No, he never hit me. But he left fingerprint bruises on my arms a few times because he didn't believe my explanations. If I spent too long at the grocery store, he accused me of sneaking off to see someone else. He even started pressuring me not to travel on the weekends with my father, unless he went along." She straightened again. "So, frankly, I was afraid to stay even another day. In fact, the night before I quit, I packed a suitcase and moved in with my father and stepmother for a couple of weeks, until I could have all the locks and security codes changed at my town house."

His stare became even more searching as he studied her. She held her breath and returned his gaze without blinking. Let him see the truth in her face. If he needed something else to convince him, she would even detail the dishonest business practices, though she had told David she wouldn't. He hadn't kept his promise not to trash her reputation out of vindictiveness, had he?

"You didn't even take your last paycheck." Brent's words were slow, thoughtful.

"I didn't want anything else to do with David or his company. I didn't need the money, and taking any more from him would have made me feel dirty."

An instant of understanding dawned on his face, replaced almost immediately by more suspicion. Though she'd been entirely truthful, he still didn't believe her.

"I can understand you not needing the money, especially when you have so much. In fact, just last week you must have gotten a bonus of some kind. Fifty thousand dollars worth." His head turned as he looked purposefully at the box in the corner. When he faced her again, his lips were tight. "You have to admit, that looks pretty suspicious since we just found a box of cash addressed to you. Detective Gaines is going to want an explanation."

Her mouth felt stuffed with wool. How had he found out about that fifty-thousand-dollar deposit? He'd been checking her out pretty thoroughly, which meant he must suspect her of being involved with Frank. Indignant anger stiffened her spine—how dare he?

But almost immediately, the anger dissolved. He was her boss, after all, and he'd flown all the way to Vegas to help her. The situation did look bad, even she could see that. First Brent found out she had a relationship with someone at work, which is exactly what that detective accused her and Frank of. Then the discovery of that box of money. And now the deposit.

That stupid fifty thousand dollars! Why had she accepted it? If she didn't do some fast explaining, that money was going to land her in jail for murder.

EIGHT

Brent saw Lauren wince, and disappointment stabbed through him. She *was* hiding something about that money.

He completely accepted her explanation about the job at SofTech. As she talked, he'd watched her closely, on high alert for signs of deception. What he saw was a pair of clear green eyes, an open expression and a lovely, if slightly trembling, mouth. That jerk of an ex-boss had lied to Mason, either out of bitterness or to cover up any hint of his own shady business practices. By the sound of things, she got away from him just in time. The behavior she described was exactly how an abuser operated—he became gradually more controlling, more suspicious, more physical.

But Brent's mention of that fifty-thousand-dollar deposit made her uncomfortable. Was she involved in illegal activities?

"Fifty thousand dollars is a lot of money." He studied her face and saw another slight wince at a second mention of the money. "Under normal circumstances I wouldn't dream of asking about it." He waved a hand toward the boxed computer in the corner. "These are not normal circumstances."

Her throat moved as she swallowed, and her shoulders rose with a deep breath. "It was a gift from my father."

Oh, come on, girl! You can do better than that.

Skepticism must have shown on his face, because she nodded with vigor. "Really, it was. My birthday was last week, and Daddy wanted to give me a new car. He and my stepmother are spending the month at their villa in Italy, so he couldn't give it to me in person. Instead he transferred the money into my account."

"Fifty thousand dollars for a car?" He squinted at her. "What kind of car are you getting?"

A flush stained her cheeks, but she answered without hesitation. "A Mercedes-Benz C-class 300."

With an effort, he stopped his jaw from dropping. A twenty-four-year-old business analyst driving a Mercedes?

"I know what you're thinking." She squirmed in her seat. "It's true. I'm the spoiled daughter of a rich man." Her body tilted forward as she looked him straight in the face. "I'm trying to become self-sufficient, I really am. I'm paying my own bills now, buying my own clothes. When Daddy told me he wanted to give me a car for my birthday, at first I said no. I can get a loan and buy my own car. But…a Mercedes?" Her shoulders gave an apologetic shrug. "Who can pass that up?"

Okay, yeah, she had a point. If someone offered to give him a free luxury car, he'd have a hard time saying no himself. And the existence of an overly indulgent, wealthy father actually explained the fact that she'd walked away from her final paycheck at SofTech. What could it have been, a thousand dollars? Maybe fifteen hundred? Who needed that when Daddy was made of money?

She reached toward him, as though to place her hand on his arm, but then stopped inches before she touched him. Her fingers hovered in the space between them for a moment, then her hand returned to her lap.

"Please believe me, Brent. I don't know anything about that computer." Her eyes moved as her gaze slid to the corner and then back to his. "Frank was obviously into something that wasn't on the up-and-up, and he was trying to involve me. I have no idea why."

Tears sparkled in her eyes, and Brent had to steel himself against the urge to reach out and draw her into a comforting embrace. Instead, he propelled himself out of the chair and paced to the opposite end of the room. He couldn't look at her and think at the same time.

Lord, I believe her. But I need to keep a level head here, and I don't trust myself. You know the truth. Could You help me out?

The silence in the room drew out as Brent weighed Lauren's explanations. She remained quiet behind him, but he felt tension radiate from her in nearly palpable waves. Gradually, his doubts eased and a sense of peace crept over him. His tight fists relaxed. He believed her. Call it divine guidance or gut instinct, but he felt good about his decision. Whatever it took to help her out of this mess, he was prepared to do it.

He turned to face her. "All right. As soon as we get through with this workshop, we'll start trying to discover what Frank was into, and why he wanted to involve you."

Her rigid posture relaxed visibly and she sagged against the back of the chair. She opened her mouth to speak, shut it and swallowed. Then she cleared her voice and tried again. "Thank you, Brent. I can't tell you how relieved I am that you believe me."

A tender wave flooded him. She looked so small sitting there on the front row of this huge room. So alone in the sea of empty chairs. She *was* in a highly vulnerable position. If Mason could dig up those two suspicious pieces of information in such a short time, it wouldn't be long before Detective Gaines discovered the same.

"We'll figure it out." His words were voiced as much to convince himself as to comfort her.

"So as you can see, Sterling Foods had an urgent business need to update the order-entry system, and it had to be done quickly." Lauren let her gaze sweep the tops of the heads of the audience. If she looked lower, at their faces, her shaky knees threatened to dump her on the floor.

Almost every chair was taken for the session. That actually made it easier to get through her presentation, because she could let her eyes unfocus. The audience turned from nearly two hundred faces to a single vague whole, one person indistinguishable from the next. It was much easier to speak to an anonymous group than a whole bunch of individuals.

With iron resolve, she allowed herself to turn her head and glance toward the corner behind her. The presence of that computer full of cash hovered like an unseen monster in the room. They needed to hand it over to the police as soon as possible, no matter what Brent said.

She flipped the last page of her presentation document on the podium. "And now, I'm going to turn the floor over to Sterling Foods' Vice President of Information Technology, Brent Emerson."

Brent rose from his chair in the front row and headed toward the table where they'd set up the server for the demo. Lauren left the podium to go to the smaller table where she would operate the notebooks. Brent gave her a huge smile.

"Good work," he whispered when they passed each other.

His praise sent a thrill coursing through her. Not only was he her boss, but in the past few hours she'd started to feel her respect building for him as a man. She lifted her head higher and took her seat with confidence.

He picked up the handheld microphone and strode confidently to the center of the room. "How many of you have a business need similar to Sterling Foods'? I'd like to hear from a few of you." A number of hands shot up, and Brent made his way to a woman nearby. "Tell me a little about your project."

Lauren watched, impressed, as he worked the crowd. She hadn't done too badly, but she'd stayed behind the podium, even had found herself clutching the wooden edge tightly a couple of times. Brent, on the other hand, engaged the crowd as he walked among them. His manner was so easygoing, so confident, that the energy level in the room rose considerably as he spoke.

He really is an aberration. Technical, intelligent and dynamic in front of a crowd. And heart-stutteringly handsome, too.

The thought came so suddenly it startled her. She picked up a pen from the table and rolled it between her fingers, only half listening to Brent's conversation with the conference attendees. Just because she admired him professionally did not mean she could allow herself to think of him as handsome. In fact, she'd been battling a sense of guilt since he agreed to help her. Did that mean her resolve to stand on her own had weakened?

But surely taking care of herself didn't mean she could never accept help from anyone, ever again.

To distract herself, she scanned the crowd seated before her. Since their attention was focused on Brent, who still stood among them but had begun to detail the technical aspects of Sterling Foods project, she felt no anxiety studying their faces.

Actually, many of them had a similar look. These days computer professionals came in all shapes and sizes, but there were still a fair number of nerdy-looking young men with oversize glasses, pasty white complexions and ties that looked more like nooses knotted around their long necks. Most of them carried laptops or smart phones, and tapped feverishly as they listened to Brent talk.

One slender young man in an aisle seat in the center of the room took no notes. He did not wear the intently fascinated expression that many of the other attendees did, but sat with his hands folded calmly in his lap. Something about him looked vaguely familiar, but Lauren couldn't place his face. Had she seen him in the hallway earlier? On the other hand, his features were unremarkable, almost nondescript. He probably just had one of those common faces that looked like those of a dozen other people.

His head turned, and his gaze met hers. His lips lifted in a slight smile, a stranger's acknowledgment, before he looked back at Brent. Feeling as though she'd been caught staring, Lauren looked away.

Her eyes were drawn to a face in the back row, where her gaze locked onto someone staring directly at her. Shock coursed down her spine. This face she knew, all too well.

David.

What is he doing here?

The intensity darkening his eyes smacked her from across the room. Her heartbeat pounded as though struggling against a sudden crushing weight. Even from this distance, she saw the square set of his jaw, the tight lips. He looked as though he hated her.

It was all Lauren could do not to leap up from the table and run from the room.

NINE

"During the test phase of the project, we uncovered a couple of bugs that gave us some serious problems." As Brent spoke, he headed toward the table where he'd set up the computer to emulate a server. "Those problems did cause an unanticipated delay, which didn't go over well with the steering committee." He flashed a wide grin around the room. "But you all know how stuffy those executives can be." The crowd laughed at his self-deprecation.

He slid the microphone into the stand on the table and angled it toward his face so he could use both hands on the keyboard. The screen overhead was black, waiting for him to pull up the server and press the keys that would display his computer and Lauren's.

"What I'd like to do now is walk you through the application, so you can see both the technical side and the user interface."

He glanced across the room to see if Lauren was ready on her end. She wasn't looking at him, or even at her notebook screen. Instead, she stared out into the audience, her eyes wide and her lips pinched. The muscles in her neck corded with tension. Brent gazed out into the crowd but couldn't see anything that might have alarmed her.

He directed his voice toward her. "Just give me a minute to pull up the database-monitoring software, and Ms. Bradley will enter a sample transaction."

At the mention of her name, her head jerked toward him. Round eyes above hollow cheeks locked on to his face. What had come over her? Was that fear he saw in her face? He raised his eyebrows in an unspoken question.

Her lips tightened, and her head tilted sideways. Whatever message she was trying to send remained a mystery. Brent lifted his shoulders in an almost-shrug and shook his head. With a jerky nod and a sigh, she seemed to get control of herself. Her fingers began tapping on the keyboard.

He grabbed his mouse and clicked a series of icons to display the set of files Frank had labeled Vegas. Just before he double-clicked the program for his demo, a file snagged his gaze.

Wait a minute. What was this? A file he hadn't seen before lay at the top of the list. The file detail reflected a date modified of today and a time of about ten minutes ago. But how could that be? This computer hadn't been out of his sight in over an hour, and he hadn't touched that file. He moved the mouse pointer to hover over the entry. The author of the file was listed as Labetti.

Lauren's voice cut through his thoughts. "I'm ready when you are."

With an effort, Brent forced himself to open the workshop program and continue with their session. But as soon as they got through this demo, he intended to check out that file.

* * *

Throughout the demonstration part of their workshop, David's glowering stare remained fixed on Lauren. She felt the heat radiating toward her as though she were standing near a fireplace. After the initial shock, the reason for his presence at an international technology conference became obvious. He owned a software-development company. Part of the business' success required that he and his staff stay on top of developing trends in the industry. But that didn't explain why he would attend *her* workshop. His reason couldn't be interest in the subject, because his business wasn't in an industry that would use an order-entry system like this one. Which meant he came here for one reason— to intimidate her.

She did her best to ignore his glare and limited her selection of hands-on volunteers to other areas of the large conference room. Whenever she turned her back in his direction, she felt as though daggers were being thrown at her. Tense knots in her stomach grew tighter with every minute that passed.

To make matters worse, Brent was apparently feeling the stress, as well. Though he'd lost none of his professionalism during this last part of the workshop, he rushed through the question-and-answer session. He still answered all the participants' questions, but his short sentences and rapid-fire words made it obvious he was in a hurry. That suited her just fine, since the quicker this session ended, the sooner David would leave. But why was Brent rushing? Had he seen David in the audience?

Finally, the workshop time drew to a close. With a quick mouse click, Brent closed down the projection display.

"All right, folks. That's all we have time for." Relief flooded his tone and the smile he swept over the room. "Thanks for coming. If you have any more questions, feel free to email me or Ms. Bradley after the conference."

A polite applause filled the room. Lauren couldn't manage a smile as their audience began filing through the doors to head to their next sessions. Now was the danger time. Would David approach her? What if his intent was to do more than simply intimidate her? Nerves taut, she left the notebooks on the table and hurried across the room to where Brent still sat at the other table. Surely her ex wouldn't try anything within hearing distance of Brent.

Brent glanced up at her for only a second, then returned his attention to the computer monitor. "Hey. I think I found something important." He spoke quietly so as not to be overheard by the attendees filing through the main doors on their way to their next session.

Standing in relative safety at his side, Lauren risked a glance toward the rear of the room. David had left. She almost collapsed into the chair next to Brent. Thank goodness.

"You are not going to believe who was in this room." She kept her voice at a whisper, as well.

Brent didn't look away from the computer monitor, his fingers busy on the keyboard. "Yeah? Who?"

"David Reynolds." Lauren swallowed hard. Even the sound of his name on her lips left tendrils of anxiety.

Brent shot her a quick look. "Seriously? I'm surprised he had the nerve to show up here."

"Trust me, he has lots of nerve." She studied his face, noted the tight line his lips formed as he concentrated on the computer in front of him. "You didn't see him?"

"Wouldn't know the guy from Adam. Never met him."

So David wasn't the reason for the sudden tension in Brent during the session. She looked at the computer monitor, curious about what demanded such concentration. On the display was a list of files. The file names, she noted, were nothing but a string of numbers. She wasn't a computer novice, but these file types weren't familiar at all. Definitely technical stuff.

"You said you might have found something?"

He nodded. "I'm not sure what it is yet, but it's definitely Frank's work. Looks like when we activated the network for our demonstration, this computer opened a protected connection to the internet and began receiving data."

"Really?" Lauren straightened and looked again at the screen. "Can you tell who it's coming from?"

"No." His jaws bulged as his teeth clenched. "They're definitely database transactions, but they're encrypted and password protected. It's a pretty sophisticated encryption code."

A pair of conference attendees stood near the rear doors talking to each other. Though they spoke quietly, the room's acoustics carried the drone of their voices to Lauren in the front. She watched as Brent's fingers tapped the keyboard, and the screen filled with unintelligible data. Brent leaned forward, studying what looked like a bunch of gobbledygook to her.

As if this day wasn't bad enough. Frank's death. Being questioned by that stern detective. The blackjack dealer. The money. Her first public presentation. David. She could feel tension knotting the muscles in her neck and sending stabs of pain into her skull. Her fingers kneaded at the knots. She should get started packing up their equipment. The room would be needed in an hour.

"I sure could use a cup of hot tea," she murmured, more to herself than to Brent.

"I'm sure the conference has refreshments set up somewhere for the attendees." He didn't look away from the screen to answer.

True, and for a nanosecond she considered going to look for them. A stab of fear made her head throb. "I'm not setting foot outside of this room by myself. Not only is my ex-boss here, but there's also a killer on the loose."

The words left her mouth, followed immediately by a disturbing thought. *What if they're one and the same?*

No, that was a ridiculous notion. David was dishonest and controlling, but she couldn't imagine any scenario where he would kill someone.

"There's a kitchen area just a few doors down that hallway." Brent nodded toward the access door to the left of the giant projection screen. "They had coffee, so they probably have tea, too. It's a private access corridor for the conference staff. When I was out there, I didn't see a soul."

The thought of leaving the room alone, even though a private hallway, left her cold. Then she felt foolish. Once again, she was hovering around a guy for protection. If she was afraid to walk a few yards by herself to get a cup of tea, she really was a sniveling, dependent little girl.

She put a hand on the table and pushed herself upright. "Okay. You want me to bring you something?"

Distractedly, he mumbled, "Yeah, water would be good."

When she got to the door, she hesitated. What if

David had found the rear exit and was waiting to get her alone? The door was thick, probably soundproof, and swung closed automatically. If she got into a struggle, Brent would never hear her.

Feeling like a wimp, she retrieved one of the small laptop boxes and used it as a wedge to prop the door open. There. Now if she screamed, she'd be heard.

On second thought, if David Reynolds tried to approach her, she would hold nothing back. They'd hear her scream in every casino up and down the Strip.

TEN

The encryption code Frank had used was impressive. Brent tried every trick he knew to crack into the numbered files, but nothing worked. Frustrated, he accessed Sterling Foods' main servers through the internet connection and typed the commands to start an automatic code generator process. It would probably take hours, if not days, but eventually he would crack Frank's code.

He'd barely finished keying in the last command when one of the main doors swung open with a bang. Detective Gaines, tailed by two uniformed Las Vegas police officers, entered the room.

"Where is Ms. Bradley?"

He barked the question like a command, which immediately set Brent's teeth together. Did the man take lessons in offensive behavior? If he intended to force Brent's cooperation by assuming an obnoxiously superior attitude, he failed. In fact, Brent felt his hackles rise.

"She's not here."

The detective strode down the center aisle of empty chairs, his expression settling into a smirk. "I can see that. Where is she?"

Brent considered his response. He didn't want to lie.

That rubbed like sandpaper against his beliefs. But neither could he put Lauren in this man's control.

"She was really uptight after our presentation and needed a break." Completely true. A search for tea counted as a break, didn't it?

"So she went back to her room?"

Brent struggled to come up with a way to answer truthfully. Instead, he shrugged.

Gaines arrived at the computer table and stood on the other side, towering over him. If his glare was meant to be intimidating, he succeeded. Brent found himself fighting not to look away, a sure indication of deception.

After a moment, the detective's expression became speculative. "Mr. Emerson, I'd like to share something with you, something we've uncovered."

Had the guy dug up a record of Lauren's birthday gift from her father? Or had he, like Mason, spoken with the insidious David Reynolds?

"What might that be, Detective?"

"We ran a trace on Ms. Bradley's recent passport activity. Seems she's spent a lot of time out of the country in the past six months. France. Italy." He paused, then spoke with purpose. "Costa Rica."

Brent's thoughts kicked into high gear. Frequent international travel did look suspicious, because the average American couldn't afford it. But Lauren was the daughter of a wealthy world traveler.

"She told me her father is spending the month at their villa in Italy." He shrugged. "The guy must have money, and I guess he likes to take his daughter with him on his travels. There's no law against that, is there?"

The detective's expression went stony. "Perhaps not.

But guess who has also been in Costa Rica within the past six months?" He leaned across the table and placed his face inches from Brent's. "The victim, Frank Labetti."

Brent jerked back in his chair, shocked. "Lauren went to Costa Rica with Frank?"

Gaines's head shrugged sideways. "It doesn't look like they were there at exactly the same time, but it's still suspicious."

A laugh eked out of Brent's lungs. "Come on, Detective. Are you going to question every American who visits Costa Rica?"

The man's lips pursed as he let the question pass unanswered. "The other piece of evidence we uncovered is more compelling." He rounded the table and, uninvited, slid into the empty chair that Lauren had vacated moments before. Sitting sideways on the seat, he faced Brent full-on. "We haven't recovered the murder weapon yet. But we did discover an interesting tidbit of information. Two weeks ago in a gun shop just outside Atlanta, a woman purchased a handgun with a silencer. The gun shop's records indicate the buyer's name was Lauren Bradley."

A block of cement formed in Brent's gut. The weight glued him to his chair. He couldn't have moved if he'd wanted to. There had to be some mistake. Was Lauren a gun collector, maybe? But if that were true, why buy a silencer?

The image of her face, those clear eyes, hovered in his mind. He couldn't believe she'd deceived him. He wouldn't believe it.

"Listen, Detective." He leaned forward and forced the man to meet his gaze. "I can't explain that, and I'm not even going to try. But I do know that Lauren didn't kill Frank. I'd stake my career on that. Something strange is going on here. People keep accusing her of doing things she swears she didn't do. I believe her. Someone is trying to frame her."

The man snorted and shook his head with disgust. A hand rose to pinch the back of his neck as he gave Brent a pitying stare. "She's got you fooled, Mr. Emerson."

Brent's spine stiffened. "I don't think so, Detective Gaines."

He endured a long moment under the man's piercing gaze. Then Gaines slapped his hands on his thighs and rose.

"Regardless of your opinion, I've got enough circumstantial evidence to take her in for questioning. So where is she?"

Brent went still. His response formed in his mind, the words carefully noncommittal.

"She was very tense and said she needed to relax. You might try her hotel room."

Gaines held his gaze for the span of three breaths, then gave a curt nod. "I'll do that. And if you see her first, I'm sure you'll let her know I'd like to speak to her, won't you?"

Brent answered absolutely truthfully. "Of course, Detective. As soon as I see her."

With one more weighty stare, Gaines strode out of the room, the two officers on his tail. Not until the door closed behind them did Brent allow himself to sag against the chair back.

The paper tab from the tea bag dangled over the rim of the coffee cup in one of Lauren's hands. In the other she carried a glass of ice water for Brent. The only people she'd seen in this back hallway were a pair of women in serving aprons wheeling a cart loaded with pitchers of ice water and glasses. Not a sign of David lurking around, thank goodness.

As she neared the door she'd propped open with a box, Brent's voice reached her ears.

"She told me her father is spending the month at his villa in Italy."

Lauren stopped. Who was Brent talking to about her? Had David returned to find her? She shrank against the wall and slid slowly toward the door, halting just outside.

"Guess who has also been in Costa Rica within the past six months?" A pause. "The victim, Frank Labetti."

She knew that voice. Not David, but Detective Gaines. He'd come back to question her some more. A shudder threatened. Another session with the bullying detective? Her nerves were so frazzled she couldn't handle that right now.

Then his words penetrated. Frank has *also* visited Costa Rica? Why, they were talking about her! She had flown to Costa Rica a couple of months ago. Daddy had taken her and Lisa for the weekend. But Frank hadn't been there. Anger warmed the skin beneath her collar. Gaines was still trying to make it sound as if she and Frank had been having an affair.

Well, she'd just march right in there and tell him how wrong he was. She heaved herself off the wall in preparation to stepping through the doorway.

The next words that drifted to her stopped her cold.

"The gun shop's records indicate the buyer's name was Lauren Bradley."

A violent trembling took possession of her body. Hot tea sloshed out of the cup and burned her fingers.

Moving carefully, she knelt and set the cup and glass on the floor, but once she was down on her haunches she lacked the strength to rise again. Her legs were shaking too badly to support her.

They thought she'd bought a gun. But she hadn't! So how could some gun shop in Atlanta have her name?

Did Frank somehow falsify those records? He must have done so. He, or someone he was working with. Maybe even the person who shot him. The sheer volume of the evidence against her proved someone was intent on pinning Frank's murder on her. This was not just someone covering their tracks. No, they wanted *her* personally.

A ragged breath shuddered into her lungs as the realization hit her. There was no other explanation. But why? She'd never harmed anyone.

Except David.

"No." The word came out as a whisper and made barely more noise than a silent footfall on thick carpet.

She hadn't done anything to David except leave him. Surely he wasn't vindictive enough to want her to go to prison for that. The memory of the weight of his glare during the workshop hit her anew. She'd felt menace in that glare, maybe even hatred.

A different sound came from the conference room, the metallic click of a door closing. Breath trapped in her lungs, Lauren strained to hear sounds in the room. There were none.

Using the wall to support her, she rose. Did Brent still believe her, even after hearing more false evidence? What if she entered the room and he started calling for Gaines to return?

That was a risk she had to take. What other option did she have? She was alone in a strange and frightening place, and Brent was the one person who had actually listened to her protestations of innocence.

Fighting against a sudden rush of tears, she pushed the door open farther and stepped over the box she'd used to wedge it. Her gaze flew to Brent, who still sat in his chair in front of the computer, only now his arms hung limp at his sides. She couldn't read his expression.

"Brent, I didn't go to Costa Rica with Frank, and I've never bought a gun in my life." Tears blurred her vision, and she blinked them away so she could see him clearly. "Please. You've got to believe me."

ELEVEN

His thoughts caught in a giant whirlpool, Brent could only stare at the pretty young woman in front of him. Tears left a wet trail down each cheek. Her eyes begged him to trust her. His heart gave a lurch behind his rib cage.

Now that Gaines no longer sat in front of him with that arrogant, accusing expression, the evidence he'd uncovered couldn't be ignored. How easy was it to forge the records in a small gun shop?

Lord, this is looking bad, really bad.

He needed to give Mason a call and relay the latest developments. Surely a P.I. who had the connections to access private financial records could also dig something up from a local shop owner. Of course, he knew what Mason would say when he called. The same thing his sister Emily would say if she knew of this situation. That he was an idiot, and he was lousy at telling the truth from a lie.

But God wasn't.

Lord, please stop me from doing anything stupid. Am I being deceived? Taken in by the pretty face of a killer?

As he weighed the question in his soul, a sense of

certainty stole over him. His instincts still told him that Lauren wasn't dishonest. No matter how incriminating the circumstances, he still believed that she was innocent.

He rose and crossed the room to put a hand on each of her arms, feeling the violent emotions that trembled through her body. With a dip of his head, he forced her to look at his face.

"Listen to me. I said I believed you, and I do. I can't tell you not to worry, because I'm worried, too. But we're going to figure this out, okay?"

Her face crumpled as she gave way to tears. Without a thought, Brent pulled her forward and wrapped her in a strong embrace. Company policy had no place here. This woman needed whatever comfort he could give her. Sobs wracked her body, and her arms crept around his waist. His shirt grew wet with her tears.

When her sobs slowed, he lifted a hand and stroked the back of her head. Soft, silky blond hair surrounded his fingers. Gently, he tilted her head back until she was looking up at him. Fresh tears spilled over her lashes and wet her cheeks. He raised his other hand, cupped her face and wiped the tears away with his thumbs. Thinking only to offer comfort, he dropped a soft kiss onto her forehead, much as he would give his sister Emily.

Only the contact of his lips against her skin was not sisterly in the slightest. Shock vibrated through his body. Lauren must have felt it, too. Her eyes widened, and her mouth opened slightly as she gasped.

Without wasting time to consider his actions, he covered those sweet lips with his own.

It felt so right, so safe, within the circle of Brent's strong arms. Lauren melted into the kiss, her knees going weak again, this time for an entirely different reason.

Wait! What am I doing?

Reality broke over her like a thunderclap. This was her *boss*. Had she learned nothing from the disaster with David?

She broke the kiss, unwrapped her treacherous arms from around his waist and pushed away from him.

"I…I can't." Sobs were still very close to the surface, and she had to swallow one back in order to speak.

A hurt expression flashed across his features. His arms, a moment ago so strong and warm around her, fell like weights at his side.

She couldn't stand to see pain in the eyes trained on her. "I'm sorry, Brent. I just can't do this, not again." His brows jumped upward, and she rushed to explain. "I know you're nothing like David. That's not what I'm saying. It's just that…" She wrapped her arms around her middle and squeezed, searching for words to convey her feelings. She came up blank. At the moment, she had no idea what she was feeling beyond the tingling that lingered on her lips.

Brent raised a hand to scrub at his scalp and averted his eyes. "You're right. I'm the one who should apologize. Besides jeopardizing both our jobs, I shouldn't take advantage of you when you're in a vulnerable state. Only a jerk would do that."

She raised a hand in protest. "You're not a jerk. You're…" A lump lodged in her throat. She couldn't tell him what she thought of him, how she admired his intelligence and strength and the commanding presence he exuded. If she did, she'd find herself in his arms again before she could stop herself.

Instead, she lowered her hand to her side. "Can we just pretend that didn't happen?"

He raked his fingers through his hair. "Yeah. Of course. That's what we need to do." With jerky movements, he crossed the room to the computer he'd been working on when she left the room. "We need to get this stuff packed up and figure out what to do with that." He nodded toward the cash-filled computer.

Lauren choked back a surge of disappointment that she didn't want to analyze. There was no future in a relationship with him.

In fact, she might not have a future at all, if they didn't get this situation resolved soon.

She cleared her throat. "Did you figure out anything about those updated files from the internet?"

"Not yet." He shut down the server and leaned over the table to begin disconnecting cables. "I've got a code-cracking routine running on Sterling's main servers. Hopefully that will uncover the encryption soon. In the meantime, I'd like to take this computer up to my room so I can keep working on it."

"What about that one?" Lauren glanced at the box in the corner.

He straightened from his work to stare at it. "We can't leave it here, and I don't feel comfortable about taking it in either of our rooms. What about asking the casino's manager if we can store it in their safe?"

Lauren gaped at him. "You mean tell them about the money?"

"No, they'll just assume that the computer has some highly sensitive corporate information on it."

Doubt assailed her. Would it be considered obstruction of justice if they didn't turn the money over to Detective Gaines immediately? But if they did, he would take her to jail.

"It'll only be for a few hours," Brent assured her as he returned to his task of unhooking the server. "I'm not suggesting we keep the money or anything like that, but there's something about that Gaines guy that rubs me the wrong way. What I'd like to do is call Sterling Foods' corporate attorney and ask him for a referral to a lawyer out here. We need some legal counsel before we do anything else."

His plan made sense. Gaines certainly did rub Lauren the wrong way, too, and contacting an attorney sounded like wise advice.

"Okay," she agreed. "Let's get everything packed up and we'll pay a visit to the casino manager."

A tiny bit of tension seeped out of the taut muscles in her neck. At least they knew their next step. They weren't running completely blind anymore.

Brent cracked open the door at the end of the service corridor and stuck his head through. The next conference session had not yet finished, so the convention center's hallways were sparsely populated. A few attendees loitered here and there, talking with each other, tapping on their computers while seated at tables put there for that purpose. He saw no sign of Gaines.

"Okay, it's clear."

He pushed the door open wider with his back so Lauren could step through, the hollowed-out computer held firmly in his hands. She carried the server, which was much smaller and lighter than the ancient, clunky one. The rest of the equipment he had returned to the storage closet while Lauren stayed out of sight in the private kitchen.

They fell into step side by side. "I still think we're going to draw too much attention, lugging these things around."

He laughed. "You're kidding, right? We're at a technology conference. There are computers everywhere you look."

She gave him a wry smile. "Okay, you've got a point."

As they walked, he tried to study her without appearing to do so. Though outwardly calm, her face bore signs of stress in the tight skin at the corners of her eyes. Guilt stabbed him at the knowledge that he'd added to that stress.

He thrust the memory of their kiss away, along with a lingering sense of regret that a relationship with her wasn't possible. In different circumstances...

They passed through the glass-enclosed tunnel that separated the conference center from the casino without incident. As they approached the end, the musical sound of slot machines grew louder. Cigarette smoke stung his nostrils.

Brent paused just inside the casino to get his bearings. Lights of every color of the rainbow glared from a thousand sources, and it took his eyes a moment to adjust.

"There's a cashier stand over there." Her hands full carrying the server, Lauren nodded across the room.

He squinted, still scanning the room. "The manager will probably be in the administrative offices." Against the wall to their left he saw a flashing sign advertising the *Best Celebrity Impersonators on the Strip,* with an arrow indicating the direction of the casino's box office and theater. Nothing resembled management offices.

"We could ask the hotel desk clerk," she suggested.

"Good idea."

They began weaving their way through the casino toward the opposite end. Every Vegas casino operated around a certain theme. The Venetian offered gondola rides with an opera-singing Italian guide. The Paris included restaurants resembling French bistros and corridors designed like charming Parisian markets. Here at the Hollywood, they certainly made the most of the celebrity angle. Impersonators mingled with the gamblers at all hours of the day or night.

A familiar figure snagged his attention. Elvis, his arm resting on the colorful blinking lights atop a slot machine, leaned toward a female gambler with a flirty smile on his full lips. This impersonator was portraying the older, heavier Elvis as evidenced by a white silk jumpsuit, covered with dazzling rhinestones and a diamond-encrusted belt.

Beside him, Lauren stumbled to a stop. Her eyes were round as poker chips. "Look there."

Brent followed her gaze. Two more familiar figures stood near a roulette table, chatting with gamblers. Frank Sinatra's suit would look like normal attire in any setting, but Joan Rivers' flashy, low-cut dress and absurdly thick eyelashes stood out like a beacon. They struck a photographic pose, and several admirers lifted cameras and cell phones to take advantage of the moment.

"Don't tell me you want their autographs," he teased.

She gave him an uncomprehending glance, then caught sight of the celebrities. "Not them. Just beyond them, over there." Her head nodded to a location beyond, amid the blackjack tables.

His gut tightened. Definitely another familiar face,

but not one he wanted to see. Gaines stood talking to two men.

He had to get Lauren out of here before the detective saw her.

"Quick," he whispered, his feet already moving sideways.

"No, wait."

She ducked behind a bank of tall slot machines and placed the computer on the floor. Her purse dangled from a strap on her shoulder, and from it she produced a cell phone.

"What are you doing?" Brent hissed. "If he sees you, you're going to jail."

Her pale face bore evidence that she was well aware of the fact. "I recognize that man, but I can't place where."

Brent edged sideways until he could see the men talking with the detective. One was a slightly built guy with almost delicate features and short-cropped hair. The other was all too familiar. The blackjack dealer from this morning.

Uh-oh. Another piece of false evidence in Gaines's hand. He'd probably issue an arrest warrant for Lauren within a half hour.

Her phone in hand, Lauren stepped boldly out from the cover of the machines.

"Are you crazy?" He juggled the computer he carried to one arm, ready to grab her and pull her back with the other.

She waved him off. Outwardly calm, she raised her cell phone and aimed it toward the other end of the casino. Probably no one else was close enough to see how it trembled in her fingers.

Then he realized what she was doing. Between

Lauren and the detective stood the Frank Sinatra and Joan Rivers impersonators, posing for pictures. At first glance, Lauren looked like one more camera-toting tourist.

But what if Gaines didn't stop with a first glance?

Her phone clicked when she took the shot, and she immediately joined him behind the bank of machines.

"There. I got it. Now I can try to figure out where I've seen that man before."

A frustrated grunt escaped Brent's lips. Stubborn, risk-taking woman. "You should have let me take the picture."

"It's done. Let's get out of here."

She took a second to return her phone to her purse and pick up the computer. While she did, Brent watched Gaines through the crack between the machines. He said something to the blackjack dealer, who nodded and then walked away. Gaines and the other man stood together a moment longer, speaking without looking at each other. Gaines's head moved as he scanned the casino. The shorter man half faced away, looking toward the other side of the room. His lips moved in response to something Gaines said.

Suspicion erupted in Brent's mind. Something wasn't right. Why didn't they look at each other when they talked?

The next movement was so quick Brent would have missed it if he hadn't been looking directly at the pair. Detective Gaines slipped something white out of his jacket. An envelope? Quick as a flash, the item was transferred to the other man and disappeared into a trouser pocket. Without another word, the two turned and walked in opposite directions. Gaines, thank goodness, headed for the hotel lobby on the far end of the casino.

The other man strode directly toward them.

"Quick," he snapped at Lauren. "Over here."

He led her around another bank of machines that would block them from view. Thrusting her behind him, he peeked around the edge, waiting for the stranger to pass by. He did, swinging his arms nonchalantly. His pocket bulged with the contents that Gaines had given him.

When he was out of sight, Brent straightened. Beside him, Lauren remained slightly stooped, her head well below the top of the slot machines. Her arms hugged the server to her chest.

They couldn't go to the hotel desk now, or they'd run smack into Gaines. And the shorter guy had headed toward the conference center, which cut off their escape route. Both of their rooms were certainly being watched at this point.

His gaze swept the casino again. When he was sure the coast was clear, he nodded at Lauren.

"This way." He started toward the box office.

"Where are we going?" Anxiety tightened her voice as she hurried to match his long-legged stride.

"Anywhere but here."

TWELVE

Trotting at Brent's side, Lauren looked over her shoulder. No one was following them. At least not yet. Every faster-than-normal step jarred the breath out of her chest, but she didn't dare slow down and fall behind Brent. At least she'd worn sensible shoes today instead of heels.

They rounded a turn and saw the box office ahead of them, a large kiosk-style structure outlined with the same ornate molding that decorated the walls throughout the casino. Several mesh-reinforced windows punctuated each of the four sides, though only one cashier was in evidence. They saw no one else. Since it was hours before the first show of the day, the place was deserted.

"Just act like you belong," Brent mumbled sideways to her.

Lauren gulped. Easy for him to say. Confidence seemed to seep from his very pores. No doubt she looked like the nervous wreck she was.

Brent strode straight up to the window. The cashier, a bored middle-age woman with gray-streaked straight hair chopped off at her jaw line, looked up from the pages of the book lying open before her.

"Hello." Lauren marveled at Brent's easy tone. How could he sound so calm? "We're supposed to take these backstage and leave them for the technical crew."

The woman's expression remained impassive. "What are they?"

"Computers." He shrugged a shoulder. "I don't know what for. Something about a problem with the lighting during last night's show. Everything is run by computers these days."

"Ain't that the truth." The woman heaved herself out of her chair and retrieved a ring of keys from a drawer. "Even my car has a computer in it, and my husband hates it. Says it's a ploy by the auto industry to stop people from working on their own cars. Now you can't even hardly change the oil without a computer."

As she spoke, she let herself out of the ticket box. Was this actually going to work? Just walk up and say you want to go backstage, and in you go? Lauren didn't dare to move as the lady rounded the corner toward them, fiddling with the keys while she walked on thick ankles.

"I'm pretty worthless when it comes to cars, I'm afraid." Brent's smile stayed in place as she walked past them. "But you have to admit, computers can do some pretty impressive things these days."

Lauren followed behind them as they headed toward a side door she hadn't noticed. How could he carry on a conversation in such a normal tone? Weren't his nerves about to jump through his skin, as hers were?

"That's true," the woman admitted. "Look at the dancing fountains in front of the Bellagio. Beautiful, and all done with computers."

She selected a key and slid it into the lock. Brent glanced at Lauren over the woman's head as she turned the key and plunged the heavy steel handle downward. Lauren bit down on the tip of her tongue. Would she insist on following them in and watching them deliver the computers?

The cashier pushed the door open and flipped a switch on the inside wall. Dim lights illuminated a long, narrow corridor.

The woman pointed. "The stage manger's office is down there on the right. It's probably locked up, and I don't have a key. I'm guessing they'll be okay if you just set them down in front of his door."

"Yes, ma'am. That's what we'll do. Thank you."

Without a backward glance, Brent took off down the corridor with a determined stride, as though he didn't expect anyone to follow. The woman hesitated, the activity on her fluid features clearly indicating that she was considering following him anyway.

Quickly, Lauren stepped past her and flashed a smile of thanks as she trailed after Brent. She didn't trust her voice to speak. Instead, she tried to follow Brent's advice and act confidently, as if she belonged. Maybe the lady would leave them alone.

It worked.

"This door opens from the inside," she called after them. "I've got to get back to my window."

"Thanks again," Brent replied without turning around. "We'll just be a minute."

A metal clang from behind Lauren echoed down the corridor. She glanced backward. The cashier had left.

She hurried to catch up with Brent. "I can't believe she let us in." The bare walls carried her whisper down the narrow corridor.

"Most of the time, if you act like you have every right to be there, people won't question you." He glanced sideways at her. "Sort of like you taking that picture. Which was a pretty risky thing to do, by the way. If Gaines had seen you, he would have hauled you to jail for sure."

A shudder rippled through Lauren. The last thing she wanted to do was visit the Las Vegas jail—not even as a visitor, but especially not as an inmate.

"Probably not the smartest thing I've ever done," she conceded, "but when I saw that man talking to the detective and the dealer, I couldn't help it. He attended our workshop, you know."

"He did?"

She nodded. "I thought at the time he looked familiar, but I couldn't place where. I still can't. But maybe looking at this picture will prompt a memory."

They neared the end. A doorway on their right was labeled in large words Stage. Ah. So this hallway ran the length of the auditorium. Performers probably used it to get from the lobby to backstage before, or even during, a performance. Just ahead, the walls opened up into a cramped backstage area. Racks of clothing stood everywhere, and huge full-length mirrors were placed at either end. The only light came from the red letters of an illuminated Exit sign above a door in the far corner. Another closed door was on the other side of the room, painted white letters identifying it as the stage manager's office.

"This is great. Perfect." Brent set the computer he carried on the wooden plank floor and started flipping through the clothes on the nearest rack. "We only have a few minutes before that cashier comes to find out where we are, so we have to move quickly. Here. Put this on. We're going to disguise ourselves."

He tossed a trench coat in her direction and dashed to the next rack.

Lauren set the server down and picked up the coat. "But these are costumes, Brent. Surely you're not suggesting that we dress like Elvis and march through the casino in the open."

"Of course not. We just need a few things, not a whole costume. Here. Try this."

Something else sailed through the air. She reached up and snagged it. Her fingers tangled in the long, dark tresses of a wig. She recognized the style immediately.

"I am *not* dressing like Cher," she informed him. "Besides, when we walk through that door in disguises, don't you think that lady out there will be a little suspicious?"

Brent straightened and gave her an exasperated look. "We're not going out that way. Come on. Hurry."

He disappeared behind a rack of costumes, and Lauren immediately saw his intent. Of course. How stupid of her. The glowing red sign clearly pointed out their exit route.

Quickly, she jerked on the wig and began shoving blond strands beneath it. The trench coat wasn't too baggy, but would she draw attention by wearing a coat outside on a warm Vegas day? They'd have to take the risk, because most of these costumes were on the flamboyant side and would surely draw attention.

Brent appeared with a baseball cap pulled over his head, buttoning a white dress shirt in place of the more casual blue polo he'd worn earlier. Hanging from his arms were the straps of two bulging duffel bags. He unceremoniously dumped the contents on the wooden floor. A variety of items spilled out, everything from containers of stage makeup, to hairbrushes, to shiny leather belts.

He tossed one of the empty bags in her direction. "Put the server in here. We'll be less conspicuous carrying a bag."

She did as he requested while he stooped over the larger computer. Her purse fit inside the bag, too. One less thing to carry. She zipped the duffel closed just as he lifted the cover of the fake computer off, once again revealing stacks of hundred-dollar bills.

"We're not taking that computer?"

"Too noticeable." He clipped the words short as he shoveled bundles of cash into the other bag. Then he slid the cover closed on the empty computer and waved at the items littering the floor. "Hide this stuff, would you?"

Immediately Lauren discerned his intent. When that cashier came looking for them, she would see a computer in front of the stage manager's door. If nothing else looked out of place, she might assume she'd missed their exit while she was involved in her book. Or maybe she'd think they innocently left through the rear exit. Either way, she might not send up an alarm, unless they left a disheveled mess behind.

She attempted a joke as she shoved the contents of the bags beneath one of the costume racks. "Here we are in Vegas, not even gambling, and we still need to pray for a lot of luck if we're going to carry this off."

Brent paused in the act of lifting the computer hull and peered at her. "I don't believe in luck. What we need to do is pray for guidance."

His response surprised her. Pray for guidance? She'd only been joking. He must be pretty religious to make a statement like that. Funny, he didn't strike her as the type.

Before she could comment, he'd raced across the hall and set the computer in front of the stage manager's office. "Are you ready?"

"Sure." Lauren shouldered the duffel bag containing the server, scooped up two pairs of big-lens sunglasses from the jumbled surface of a small vanity and raced after Brent.

They skidded to a halt in front of the exit door. A heavy metal bar served as the handle, a warning appliquéd in red and white across the front. Emergency Exit Only. Alarm Will Sound.

They exchanged a glance.

"Maybe the alarm isn't turned on." She allowed a hopeful note to creep into her voice.

"Maybe." Brent's lips tightened, then relaxed. "We don't really have a choice."

True. She nodded.

Brent laid a hand on the bar. His shoulders rose as he drew in a breath. The sound of her pulse pounded in her ears. She clutched the strap of the duffel bag and watched him shove the bar forward.

A piercing screech filled the air. The alarm was definitely turned on.

THIRTEEN

Sunlight blinded Lauren for a moment. The high-pitched siren pierced her eardrums. She took in her surroundings in a glance. They were in a parking lot, with no one else in sight. Her sense of orientation kicked in, and she realized they were at the rear of the casino. The famous Las Vegas Strip lay behind them, on the other side of the immense Hollywood Hotel and Casino. The only people in sight were a couple weaving through the parked cars away from the building. They glanced up at the sound of the siren, but continued on their way to their car.

"Quick. The casino's security guards will be here in a second. This way."

Brent slipped a hand through her arm and jerked her sideways at a run. Lauren had no choice but to follow.

They made it the length of the building without encountering anyone. The siren's wail receded as they put more distance between them. At the corner of the building, Brent stopped and straightened. Lauren pulled up beside him, her breath coming in heaves. He peered around the edge.

"Okay, I think we're clear. Remember, act like you belong here."

He sauntered out into the open. Lauren gathered her courage, stiffened her spine and followed him.

The Hollywood's circular front drive lay directly ahead of them. Beyond a high blooming hedge, traffic sped by on Las Vegas Boulevard. The noise reduced the siren from the door into a distant whisper, easily unnoticed by anyone on this side of the building. Brent's confident stride aimed them at the casino's main entrance.

"Where are we going?" she whispered, trying to walk easily, as though she was out for an afternoon stroll. A drop of sweat slid between her shoulder blades, whether from nerves or from wearing a trench coat on a warm Nevada afternoon, she wasn't sure.

Brent didn't break stride. "My rental car is parked on the other side of the casino entrance. If we can get there, we're home free."

Lauren measured the distance between them and the far side of the building. It seemed to be double the size of a football field. The casino entrance was a bustling hub of activity. Uniformed bellmen rushed toward cars that braked to a halt beneath the deep awning, and hurried to open doors for well-dressed gamblers. A group of tourists burst through a large revolving door and made their way across the driveway toward the hustle and bustle of the Strip. Far beyond lay another parking lot much like the one they'd just left. Her spirits flagged. How would they be able to make it all that way without being noticed?

Lauren clutched the strap of the heavy duffel bag. She realized she held the sunglasses in her other hand and donned a pair. The glaring Las Vegas sun cooled in her vision. She offered the second pair to Brent, and he took it with a wordless nod of thanks.

When they entered the shade beneath the awning that covered the circular entrance, her muscles tensed to the breaking point. The glass doors leading guests into the casino were darkly tinted and allowed no glimpse of the building's interior. Could people inside see out? They inched their way past at a leisurely pace, and any moment Lauren expected to hear Detective Gaines cry, "Stop them!"

And then they were beyond the entrance. They stepped from shade into glaring sunshine as they entered the casino's south parking lot.

Beside her, Brent heaved an exaggerated sigh. "Thank the Lord. My car's just over there."

Relieved beyond words, Lauren was willing to credit the Lord with their escape, too, if that's where Brent said it came from. Her stride lengthened as she headed in the direction he indicated.

Suddenly, Brent skidded to a halt.

"Get down!"

His command resulted in her knees buckling almost without thought. She crouched down beside him, hovering between two parked cars. Moving slowly, he inched upward and stretched his neck to see over the roof. Lauren mimicked his movements.

A few rows away, a uniformed Las Vegas police officer paced between rows of parked cars.

Brent dropped down on his haunches in the cover of an El Dorado. He didn't dare speak a word to Lauren, but he didn't need to. She followed his example. Though her eyes were hidden behind sunglass, a question was clearly evident on her face. *What do we do now?*

He wished he knew.

Maybe this officer was just a security guard patrolling the Hollywood's parking lot to discourage vandals or thieves from harming the guests' cars. If so, he might not be looking for them. He removed his sunglasses and inched upward, his head cocked at an angle so he could get a look at the guy while exposing as little of his head as possible.

A patch on the uniform clearly read LVMPD—Las Vegas Metropolitan Police Department. A standard-issue service revolver was secured menacingly on the officer's wide utility belt.

Brent dropped back down to the pavement. Okay. A cop in the parking lot. Getting to the Grand Am he'd rented wasn't going to be as easy as he'd hoped. They'd have to crawl through the lot without being seen.

A tap on his arm drew his attention to Lauren. Her lips formed a rigid white line, and she pointed to another area of the parking lot. Again, Brent rose a fraction and peered in that direction.

A second police officer paced slowly down another row of cars. Brent's spirits plummeted.

The rental car is between them. They're watching it, staking out the location and waiting for us to show up.

Both officers headed away from their hiding place at the moment. Their heads turned to the right and left as they inspected the space between the cars like prison guards checking prisoners' cells after lockdown. In a few minutes they'd turn and come back this way. He and Lauren were sitting ducks.

Lord, what now? We've got to find a safe place so we can contact an attorney and figure this out. I'm out of options.

He leaned heavily against the hot metal car door, hands clutching the bag full of cash. Maybe they ought to turn themselves in. Confess everything to Gaines and pray he'd listen to their side of the story. Of course, Lauren would go to jail, but if they got an attorney, maybe it wouldn't be for long.

Beside him, Lauren watched him. She'd removed her sunglasses, and he had a hard time ignoring her anxious expression. Anxious, but did he detect a hint of trust in her eyes? She trusted him to get her out of this, to keep her out of jail. The responsibility dragged at him like hardened cement.

Wait a minute. Brent straightened as a possibility occurred to him. Mason had texted him the name and address of a guy here in Vegas. A Christian guy. Maybe he'd be willing to let them come over for a few hours, make a few phone calls and figure out their next move. A flicker of hope dissolved a tiny bit of his anxiety. This felt like a good move.

But first they had to get out of this parking lot unseen. Fast.

He signaled to Lauren that they were making a move. Her nod came quickly, and she grasped the bag containing the server in both hands. He did the same with the money bag, then inched upward again to check out the officers' locations. They were about ten rows away, a few rows beyond his rental car. That meant they would probably turn and head in this direction soon.

With a silent prayer, Brent rose to a semihunched position and ran, Lauren close behind him.

FOURTEEN

The bag containing the server wasn't heavy, but its weight dragged at Lauren's arms in this bent-over position. She dashed from the cover of the car and followed Brent across the driving lane, her stomach in her throat. Any minute one of those police officers might turn his head and see them.

When they reached the next row of parked cars, Brent slowed, glanced toward the officers and then continued. She dashed after him across another lane. Once they were safely behind a different vehicle, he stopped and dropped to a squatting position.

Lauren did the same and tried to silence her ragged breath. Where were they headed? She opened her mouth to whisper the question, and he held up a finger to stop her from speaking. The finger switched to point in the opposite direction from the officers. A movement flashed in her peripheral vision, and her pulse kicked up a notch. Were there more police over there?

A moment later, a car drove past them down the lane. Not a patrol car, but a Buick. The driver's head was turned the other way, apparently searching for a parking place.

Brent waited until the Buick passed, then raised up

again to peer toward the officers. He dropped back down and motioned for her to follow him. But instead of running toward the next row of cars, they edged around to the front of the car behind which they were hiding and crouched near the front bumper.

The officers must be coming this way. If we stay between the parked cars, they'll see us.

Bands of fear tightened around her chest. Lauren hugged the computer bag to her body and curled herself around it to make herself as small as possible. What if someone else turned down this lane looking for a parking place? There was no way they could be missed. She tucked her head and squeezed her eyes shut, unable to look. Heat radiated from the pavement and beat down on her from the sun above. Perspiration trickled down her back.

After an excruciating wait, Brent's hand tapped her shoulder. She looked into his face and saw a question etched in the lines between his eyes. He gave her a thumbs-up gesture. *Are you okay?*

Lauren bit back a hysterical laugh. Did he want a truthful answer? Instead, she managed a nod.

He gestured ahead of them. At first she thought he was simply indicating that they were ready to run across the next few parking lanes, but then she realized where he pointed. The same tall, flowering hedge that bordered the front of the Hollywood continued along this parking lot. From beyond it, the sound of traffic reached her—car engines, the occasional distant horn, the boom-boom-boom of someone's stereo speakers.

He's taking us through that hedge onto the Strip.

Wouldn't that be crowded? She glanced at her watch. Almost four-thirty. The time surprised her. In one respect, it seemed as if weeks had passed since she'd found Frank's body this morning. In another, it might have been only half an hour ago.

Four-thirty on a Tuesday afternoon in Las Vegas. Yes, the Strip was probably crowded. But what choice did they have?

She nodded to let Brent know she understood his intention, then prepared herself to run. After one more check of the police officers' location, Brent dashed across the lane. Lauren's thigh muscles protested the awkward, crouched-over posture, but she ignored the pain and followed.

He didn't stop when they reached the cover of the next row of parked cars, only glanced over his shoulder in the officers' direction as he kept running. Lauren didn't dare look. An unreasonable fear overtook her—if she turned her head, they might sense it and look back at her. Instead, she kept her gaze fixed on Brent's back and focused on matching his pace.

Three rows away, they reached the hedge. A wide, smooth sidewalk separated the parking lot from the decorative bushes. A short bank of mulched ground led up to the walkway, which stood a couple of feet above the asphalt. When they stepped up onto it, they'd be visible from the entire lot. Tension pounded in her temples. They'd be exposed.

With one final backward glance, Brent didn't even pause. He climbed the bank with one long stride and plunged right into the tall shrubbery. With a bracing breath, Lauren followed.

The hedge was planted several feet deep. Prickly limbs scratched her face, her only exposed skin. The tresses of the Cher wig became tangled in the branches, and the limbs snatched it off her head. She emerged onto a sidewalk in bright sunlight on the other side, wigless and breathless.

Six lanes of traffic rushed past a few feet in front of her. Brent stopped, his feet planted on the sidewalk, and she rammed into his back. Someone else brushed against her, and Brent bumped into someone in front of him. They were surrounded by people who were staring at them as if they'd just stepped out of a spaceship.

Great. Talk about not drawing attention to ourselves.

"Whoa, sorry about that." A light laugh accompanied Brent's words to those in their immediate vicinity. He made a show of brushing a leaf off of his white shirt and turned to her. "Now, wasn't that better than walking all the way around that hedge?"

His tone was light, almost teasing. A young man chuckled as he veered around them. Another shook his head and took his girlfriend's hand as they continued down the sidewalk. The rest of the crowd parted and flowed around them.

Brent shouldered his bag and slipped a hand beneath Lauren's arm. "Remember. Act like you belong."

She allowed herself to be propelled forward, and they blended into the moving crowd of pedestrians. The back of Lauren's neck prickled, and she had to force herself not to turn around to see if they were being followed by the police. She did look back once, when they stopped at a crosswalk, but saw nothing more alarming than a pair of ebony-clad young people draped in chains and sporting neon-pink Mohawks.

Ahead of her the famous Las Vegas Strip stretched for miles. Everywhere she looked, towers reached into the sky, and electronic billboards flashed advertisements of elaborate shows and all-you-can-eat buffets.

Fountains sprayed high, and even in the afternoon sunlight, glittering lights drew her gaze.

Brent's hand tightened on her arm. "Here comes the shuttle bus. Let's get on."

A small group of tourists stood beneath a bus stop awning just ahead. When the shuttle arrived, they surged forward. Lauren and Brent joined them and, when their turn came, climbed into the bus. Brent pulled out his wallet and gave the driver five dollars, then they made their way to a pair of empty seats. As the shuttle pulled away from the curb and merged into traffic, Lauren twisted around to look down the street toward the Hollywood Casino. She saw nothing but cars and pedestrians and flashy buildings.

A huge sigh heaved from her lungs. They had escaped.

For now.

The shuttle bus's brakes threw Brent off balance, and his arm brushed hard against the person seated on the bench next to him.

"Sorry," he mumbled.

The woman didn't even pause in her conversation with the lady on her other side. He settled the duffel bag more securely on his lap and angled toward Lauren as he slipped his cell phone from his pocket.

She leaned toward him and whispered, "Where are we going?"

"To a friend's, I hope."

Her eyebrows arched. "You hope?"

Instead of responding, he slid his finger across his phone's screen until he found Mason's number, then placed the call. Mason picked up on the second ring.

"There you are. I've been gnawing my nubs, waiting for a call. What's going on?"

Brent glanced around the crowded bus. No one was paying attention to him, but he certainly couldn't detail everything that had happened since he last spoke to his friend.

"A lot." Mason would have to be content with that for the time being. "Listen, I need another favor. Could you give your jailer friend a call? See if it's okay for us to come over."

"Us?"

Brent winced at the disapproval he heard in Mason's voice. He glanced at Lauren, whose anxious expression squeezed a place deep in his chest. "Yeah. Long story. I'll fill you in later, I promise." He lowered his voice so no one but Lauren could hear his next words. "Tell him we'd prefer not to advertise our location."

"Oh, man, oh, man. This sounds bad. You know if I have to fly out there and ID your carcass in a Las Vegas morgue, that's really going to tick me off, right?"

Despite the sarcastic jab, Brent heard worry in Mason's voice. He poured as much confidence into his response as he could manage. "Don't worry. That's not going to happen."

At least, I hope not.

"All right, if you say so." Mason didn't sound convinced. "Where are you? Still at the Hollywood Casino?"

"Not anymore." He searched the landscape through the bus's windows. "We're on the Strip, not far from the Tropicana."

"Let me give Caleb a call and I'll get right back to you."

The line went silent. He lowered the phone and looked into Lauren's anxious face.

"We're going to see a jailer?"

"He used to be a jailer. I'm not sure what he does now."

The hollows in her cheeks seemed to deepen as she received that information. "You're not sure? I thought he was your friend."

"Sort of. He's a friend of a friend."

The bus lurched to a halt, and her hands clutched the strap of the duffel bag containing the server. People left their seats to get off the bus, and others waited on the sidewalk to take their places. Lauren's eyes moved as she scanned those waiting, and she inched a fraction closer to him. Her leg trembled against his, whether from nerves or the vibration of the bus's engine he couldn't tell. Probably nerves, and who could blame her? Brent would have put a comforting arm around her shoulders, but after the intensity of their kiss earlier, he didn't dare.

His cell rang. Mason. He answered the call and jerked it to his ear. "Did you get in touch with him?"

"Yeah. Can you get to the Stratosphere in half an hour?"

Brent looked through the wide, flat windshield. The unmistakable image of the Stratosphere Tower, an icon of the Las Vegas Strip, lay a few miles ahead. This shuttle would probably take them there, or at least get them close.

"Yeah, I think we can do that."

"Good. Caleb will pick you up on the second level of the parking garage. He described his car as a piece-of-junk green vehicle with a cracked front quarter panel. Watch for him."

Another parking lot. Great.

"Will do." An unexpected knot of emotion rose to clog Brent's throat. Mason was sticking his neck out for them based on nothing more than his friendship with Brent. "I can't thank you enough, Mason."

"Oh, yes you can. I'm not sure how yet, but the payback is going to be bigger than a steak." He paused and continued in a serious tone. "You stay on your toes, hear? And call with details as soon as you can."

"I will. I promise." Brent pocketed his phone.

"This friend of your friend," Lauren said, "are you sure we can trust him?"

At this point, he wasn't sure of anything. But for her sake, he gave a confident nod and covered her clenched knuckles with his free hand. "The only thing I know about him is he's a Christian. So I'm going to say, yeah, we can trust him."

Questions formed in her eyes. She opened her mouth to speak, hesitated and then closed it again. A nod, and then she turned to stare through the window beside her.

Brent looked through the bus's front windshield at the Stratosphere Tower standing sentinel over the Strip. He sure hoped this Caleb guy was trustworthy. If not, they could be stepping into a bigger mess than the one they had just left.

FIFTEEN

The Stratosphere's eight-story parking garage was a huge concrete structure on the west side of the famous tower. The shuttle let them off in front of the casino, and Lauren followed Brent down a narrow sidewalk to the garage entrance. Pink landscaping gravel and neatly trimmed bushes lined the walkway. No big hedges to hide behind this time. Lauren cast a fearful glance behind them. No sign of the police.

They climbed the stairs to the second level. The duffel bag with the server seemed to grow heavier with every step. The ninety-degree heat lessened when they stepped into the shade of the garage, but the air smelled stale with remnants of automotive exhaust fumes. Nausea quivered in her stomach at the odor.

No, it's not the odor. I'm starving.

As if to prove the point, her stomach rumbled. When had she last eaten? It took her a moment to remember. She'd had no appetite for breakfast after the gruesome discovery of Frank's body and Detective Gaines's exhausting interrogation. She and Brent had run nonstop since then. So the last food she'd eaten was dinner with Frank last night, almost twenty hours ago. She clutched the bag's canvas handles, gritted her teeth and kept climbing.

Cars packed the second level of the parking garage behind the Stratosphere. They stepped out of the concrete stairwell, and Brent's head moved as he scanned the area.

"He's not here yet." He glanced at his watch. "I guess we'll just wait."

Lauren was suddenly too tired to answer. She backed up and leaned heavily against a round column. Shock, taut nerves and no food were taking their toll. Her limbs dragged at her body as though they had weights attached. And the heat wasn't helping. She set the bag at her feet and shrugged off the trench coat. The stale air against her bare arms felt instantly cooler.

Wait. Didn't she have something to eat in her purse? She ignored the dirty surface of the rough concrete floor, slid down the column to a sitting position and pulled the duffel bag onto her lap. Rummaging through her purse proved only mildly rewarding. She drew out a small bag of airline peanuts and a pack of gum.

"Are you hungry?" She held the peanuts toward Brent.

He turned from his intent study of the entry ramp and glanced at the package in her hand.

"Yeah, thanks." He dropped the money bag beside her and lowered himself to the ground, angled so he could see incoming traffic.

Lauren tore open the package and divided the contents—about a dozen peanuts each. When she placed the nuts in the palm of his hand, he closed his fingers to catch hers. A warm thrill danced up her arm.

"You look tired," he said. "Are you doing okay?"

Tears stung the backs of her eyes at the concern she

heard in his voice. He was such a nice guy, and look what she'd dragged him into. By all rights he ought to be irritated with her. Instead, he showed concern.

Blinking back tears, she nodded. "I am tired, but I'll be okay." Gently, she removed her fingers from his and toyed with the peanuts in her own palm. "Brent, I want to thank you for helping me. I'm sorry I've gotten you involved in this mess. I…" She paused until she could school the tremor out of her voice. "I don't know what I would have done if you weren't here."

"I do," he teased. "You'd have gone to jail for murder."

A smile twitched at the corners of his lips. Lips that had kissed her not long ago. She tore her gaze from them and shoved the memory of that kiss away.

"Seriously," Brent continued, "I can't take any credit, because we're not out of hot water yet. Not by a long shot. In fact, I've probably made things worse by encouraging you to run from the police. But I do think the Lord sent me out here to help." He leaned his head back and popped the peanuts into his mouth.

Lauren stared at him, not sure how to respond. The idea of God sending someone to help her, especially her handsome boss, was hard to believe. "Why would you say that?"

He dusted his hand against his pant leg. "Don't you think the Lord helps us when we need it?"

Actually, she had never given the idea much thought. She believed in God, but the God she knew was a remote though caring deity, someone she prayed to at night and visited at church every month or so when she wasn't traveling with her father. He watched over her. She knew that from the reverend's sermons, but she'd never considered that He might actually lend a hand.

"I guess I'm more in the camp of *God helps those who help themselves,*" she answered.

He stared at her for a long moment, unreadable thoughts running rampant across his fluid features. Finally, he answered with an uninformative, "Ah. I see."

The sound of a revving car engine bounced between the parking garage's concrete floor and ceiling. They both jerked their gazes toward the ramp. The muscles in Lauren's stomach tensed. What if it was a police car coming to get them? She scrambled to her feet and scooped up the bag containing the server. Beside her, Brent also stood and put a hand on her arm, as though ready to grab her if they had to run.

A green car rounded the corner and headed up the ramp. The front bumper lolled sideways beneath a sun-bleached hood. Lines of rust spidered through a crumpled dent in the metal in front of the passenger door.

The car screeched to a halt in front of them, and the driver's door opened. A man stood, a huge man with beefy arms and a neck like a post. His hair was gathered into a ponytail at the back of his head. He was so big, if Lauren had run into him on the street, she probably would have been afraid of him. But who could be afraid when they caught sight of the almost jolly smile that split his darkly tanned face?

He stood behind the open door, one arm resting on the hood of his car. "You Brent?"

Beside her, Brent gave a cautious nod. "And you're Caleb?"

"That I am, brother." His gaze slid to Lauren, and his grin softened. "Sorry my ride's a grimy mess. I'd have cleaned out the construction dirt if I'd known I was going to escort a pretty lady today."

Her anxiety ebbed as she looked into his face. She

couldn't recall ever seeing a more honest, open expression. Though she'd never laid eyes on this giant man before, she felt instantly that he could be trusted.

Beside her, Brent had apparently reached the same conclusion. "Before you help us, I need to tell you we're running from the police. You might get in trouble."

White teeth reappeared in the tanned face. "You wouldn't believe how often I hear that." His huge palm slapped the hood. "What are we waiting for, brother? Hop in and let's get out of here."

With less tension than she'd felt in hours, Lauren hefted her bag and followed Brent to the car. As she slid into the backseat, she realized she still clutched the peanuts in her fist. She leaned against the dusty rear seat and filled her mouth. Food had never tasted so good.

Since Lauren had climbed in the back, Brent slid into the passenger's seat. The minute he slammed the door, the car lurched forward and rounded the corner to the exit ramp. He scrambled to snap the seat belt as he was thrown against the door. The Toyota's tires squealed on the concrete floor.

"Sorry I was a few minutes late." Caleb spoke while focusing his attention through the windshield. "Had to kick a couple of guys out of the house before I could leave."

"Kick them out?" Brent eyed the man's profile. A tattoo of an elaborate cross covered the skin of his massive upper right arm, and a ponytail snaked down the back of his neck. "We're not putting you to any trouble, I hope?"

He snapped his mouth shut. What a stupid thing to say. Of course they were putting him out. If things got any worse, they might just land him in jail along with them.

"Nah, not your fault." One hand released the steering wheel to wave in a dismissive gesture. "There's always somebody crashing at my house 'cause they got kicked off someone else's couch. I don't mind. That's why I'm here." A grin creased his sun-darkened cheeks. "But I'm not stupid. I don't let them stay there when I'm gone. A crackhead will steal even cheap junk like mine if they think they can trade it for a hit."

Lauren leaned up between the front seats. "Crackhead? You let drug users stay in your house?"

He didn't hesitate. "Yes, ma'am. But only if they're sober. If they show up trashed, they're out on the streets."

The car reached the parking-garage exit. Caleb tapped the brakes to slow a fraction, then zoomed out onto the street and across oncoming traffic. They slid into a tight space in front of a car traveling in their direction, and the driver laid on his horn. Caleb merely grinned into the rearview and waved a hand at the man, as if in thanks.

A quiet choking sound came from the backseat.

"Don't worry, ma'am," Caleb told Lauren as he punched the gas pedal to pick up speed. "You gotta be aggressive here. Otherwise you'll never get anywhere. I've gotten used to the Vegas traffic in the past couple of years."

Brent's conversation with Mason came back to him. "I understand you used to be a jailer in Atlanta. What brought you to Vegas? You said something about construction?"

"That's right. Hard work, but the pay's good. But that's not what I do, it's just a means to a paycheck."

Caleb's lips pursed a second. "You might call me a missionary." A laugh barreled out of his mouth. "Yeah, that's it. I'm a missionary. Only with no funding and no resources other than these." He lifted both hands off the steering wheel long enough to splay his fingers. "So I use them to pay the bills, and trust God to do the rest."

"Mason mentioned you're a Christian."

His head bobbed a nod. "Said the same thing about you. I'm always ready to help out a brother in Christ."

Warmth seeped into Brent's chilly insides at the words.

"Apparently you help more than Christians." Lauren's dry voice crackled to the front seat.

"That's true, ma'am." Caleb glanced in the rearview mirror. "See, the Lord gave me two great big hands, and I can't believe He means me to use them just to smack people down. He wants me to give them a big old hand up, too." He settled back in his seat with a satisfied nod. "'Course, I don't mind using them to smack sense into people, either, when I need to. And when you're dealing with the people I see every day, sometimes they're just aching for a smack."

Brent laughed, and even Lauren chuckled. No wonder Mason liked this guy. Though Caleb wasn't as sarcastic as his P.I. friend, they shared a similar jabbing wit.

Caleb turned the wheel, and the car moved onto the entrance ramp for Interstate 15. When they'd crossed over to the center lane and merged into traffic, he took one hand off the wheel and rested it casually on the armrest.

"So, since you're friends and not junkies, I assume I'm offering a helping hand instead of a slap. What can I do?"

Brent scrubbed his scalp with his fingers. How much should he reveal? He felt deep in his gut that they could trust the giant man beside him, but any information they shared would only pull him deeper into the tangled mass of deception that surrounded them. The bag of money lay on the floorboard between his feet, a sobering reminder that this was no friendly visit with a new friend.

"At the moment, all we need is a place to lay low for a while, until we can sort things out and figure out our next move."

The big man's eyes narrowed as he considered this. "Without going into details, can you tell me how much trouble I could get in by helping you? Have you committed a felony?"

"Of course not," Lauren answered at the same moment Brent said, "No."

Caleb glanced sideways, and his gaze connected with Brent's. He might be a big, jovial man, but those eyes held a shrewd intelligence. They flickered toward the backseat for a fraction of a second, then returned.

He's wondering about Lauren. Mason must have spelled out his black-widow theory. Well, of course he had.

Brent twisted sideways in the seat to face him head-on. "Neither of us has committed a crime. But we need to prove that. Until we do, you could probably get in a lot of trouble by helping us."

Silence filled the car. Caleb faced forward again. His lips moved almost imperceptibly without making a sound.

He's praying. Relief flooded Brent at the realization. Without a doubt, the Lord had guided them to this man. Brent wasn't at all surprised by Caleb's answer.

"I've been in trouble before. I can handle it."

Behind him, Lauren gave a soft sigh. "Thank you."

When he turned to face the front, Brent's toe nudged the duffel bag. How had Frank gotten it, and what had he planned to do with the money? The answers lay with those computer files, of that Brent was positive. He had to crack that code, and time was running out.

SIXTEEN

The sinking sun cast long shadows across the road on Caleb's street. Lauren stared through the car's window with growing discomfort as they drove by dilapidated houses that looked to her as if they should have been condemned years before. Broken furniture and trash littered most of the yards. Caleb's Toyota looked like a luxury car compared to the heaps that lined both sides of the street.

They passed a plain two-story structure that looked like a dirty brick box with shutterless windows, apparently an apartment building. Five young men lounged on the concrete steps of the front stoop, cigarettes dangling from their mouths and beer cans in their hands. When they passed, two jerked their heads in a backward nod of greeting to Caleb, who responded the same way. Lauren sank lower in her seat.

The only distinguishing feature of the house to which Caleb drove was the absence of weeds and garbage in the sandy yard. There were even a few scraggly bushes on either side of the front door, and a collection of decorative cacti inside a scalloped border beneath the front window.

Caleb parked the Toyota in the driveway and cut the

engine. "Here we are. Home sweet home. Don't expect much, but I do keep it clean."

This was Caleb's home? Lauren managed to keep the distaste off of her face as she slid out of the car.

Don't be a prissy rich girl. Not everybody has an indulgent daddy to buy them a townhouse in a gated community.

"It's great," she assured him. "I'm thankful for it, and for your help."

Oh, how thankful she was. In his position, would she have jumped in to help a couple of strangers who were running from the police? Not a chance. Yet that's what Caleb did all the time, apparently. Helped people who were in trouble.

"Here, let me give you a hand with that."

She let him take the duffel bag from her, grateful to release her burden. When he felt the weight and noted the clearly discernable boxlike shape, questions appeared on his face. He didn't voice them but merely punched the lock button on the driver's side door and closed up the car.

"Hey, Preacher Man," called a female voice.

Lauren turned to see a pair of girls strutting down the walkway from the front door of the house across the street. They wore short skirts, low-cut blouses and unbelievably high spiked heels. Even from this distance, she could see their makeup had been thickly applied with a fondness for bright colors.

"Hello, ladies," Caleb called back to them. "You be good girls tonight, you hear?"

"We will." The answer was shouted as they got into a beat-up old car that belched smoke when the engine roared to life.

"Dancers," Caleb told them. "Both drug-free at the

moment." His eyes grew sad as he watched the car's progress down the street. "I'm praying they stay that way."

His head shook and indicated they should follow him down the driveway toward the back of the house. Moved by his obvious concern for the young women, Lauren started after him.

This guy is the real deal. He not only helps, he cares.

Brent fell in step beside her. "You doing okay?"

"Yeah." She gave him a sheepish look. "Feeling kind of humble at the moment."

He heaved a laugh. "I know what you mean. He's a great guy. I hope we don't land him in hot water."

They rounded the corner of the house. The back-yard resembled the front, nothing but sand and a few cacti along a narrow walkway leading to the back door. A round plastic table of indistinct color sat beneath a wide, peaked awning. Paint peeled on four thick wooden posts that held the sagging awning in place. Mismatched chairs were scattered around the porch, two of them occupied by men. The two Caleb had kicked out to come pick them up?

Caleb rattled his keys as he passed the pair, heading for the door. "Don't you two have anyplace to go?"

As she drew closer, Lauren saw they were both young, nothing more than boys, really. They wore dark knit hats pulled down over their ears, T-shirts, and one sported a stud in his lower lip. Smoke curled upward from the cigarettes held between their fingers.

"Nah, man," one of them answered. "Nicky said we could crash on his floor tonight, but he don't get home 'till eight."

Caleb shoved a key in the lock. "All right, you can hang around on my porch until then. But you can't stay tonight. I've got company, so I'm full up." He pushed the door open and jerked his head toward Lauren and Brent. "These are friends of mine." To them, he said, "This is Jake and Mush."

Mush? Obviously some sort of nickname.

"Hey." Brent nodded a cautious greeting toward them.

Lauren managed a smile.

"Watch your language around the lady," Caleb warned, "or I'll toss you out on your ear."

"We're good, dude." One of the boys lifted a burning cigarette toward Lauren in some sort of weird salute.

She flashed a nervous smile and hurried into the house after Caleb.

The kitchen she entered was outdated, with scarred countertops and dingy linoleum, but the faucet gleamed and the stove showed no evidence of dirt. An inexpensive table with six chairs rested beneath a light fixture in a wide breakfast nook. Lauren and Brent followed Caleb past that and entered a living area about the same size as the kitchen. A solid, square sofa sat along one wall facing an old television set on the other. Two chairs, the fabric on the arms worn, formed a semicircle around a plain wooden coffee table. A sturdy desk dominated the corner to their right, an ancient computer monitor on its scratched surface. Beige curtains were drawn closed across a double window beside the front door on the wall opposite the kitchen.

Caleb set the duffel bag containing the server on the coffee table and pointed down a short hallway. "There's two bedrooms. One just has a couple of mattresses on the floor for whomever." He looked at Lauren. "You'll take the other one, ma'am."

She opened her mouth to protest that she couldn't

take over his bedroom but then stopped. Where else would she sleep? This small house didn't offer many options. The protest died unspoken. "Thank you. And please call me Lauren."

"Lauren." Huge arms folded across his barrel chest. "Now, tell me what you need."

Lauren's mind emptied. How to answer that question? They needed information, proof that she didn't kill Frank, and Caleb couldn't give them that.

Brent took a step into the room. "If it's okay with you, I'd like to use your computer."

A shrug lifted Caleb's shoulders. "Sure, but I have to warn you. It's old and dilapidated. I don't dare keep anything newer around this place."

"That's okay. All I need is the monitor and the keyboard." He handed the duffel he carried to Lauren, then picked up the one on the table. "I brought my own box."

Caleb waved toward his desk. "Have at it, brother."

The bag of money weighed more than the server she'd been carrying. The sight of all those banded hundred dollar bills resurfaced in her mind. How much was in there? She wasn't sure she wanted to know. They'd been carrying it around for a couple of hours as though it were nothing more than a bag of clothes.

She hefted it in both hands. "Do you have someplace safe we can put this?"

"Weeeellll." Caleb scratched his jaw with a thick finger. "Safe is a relative term in this neighborhood. I don't own much I wouldn't want to lose, but I put important stuff like my tools and keys in the bedroom. There are boards in the windowsills and a lock on the door."

Lauren exchanged a glance with Brent. That would have to do. She followed Caleb's directions down the short hallway to the bedroom on the left. A king-size bed with no headboard or footboard and a four-drawer chest of drawers crowded the tiny room. A double bed would have fit much better, but a big man like Caleb probably needed the extra-long mattress. A wide leather tool belt had been dropped on the floor beside the dresser, a variety of construction tools dangling from various loops. She set the bag of money next to it.

When she returned to the living room, she found Brent crouched over the server, connecting cables to the back. He had rolled up the long sleeves of the shirt they'd taken from the dressing room at the Hollywood, and she saw the muscles in his forearms tense and roll as he worked. Her gaze traveled up his arm to the white fabric stretched across his strong shoulders. Though not as overly muscular as Caleb, Brent was every bit as fit and certainly more handsome, in her opinion.

Startled at the turn of her thoughts, she tore her gaze away and turned to find Caleb watching her. The corners of his lips tweaked with a knowing smile, and an answering blush heated her cheeks.

Before the moment became awkward, Caleb clapped his hands together. "Looks like he's going to be a while, so why don't you give me a hand in the kitchen?"

Hunger twisted in her stomach. Those peanuts hadn't gone nearly far enough. "I'm not a great cook, I'm afraid, but I'm pretty good at following directions."

"That's what I like. A woman who does what she's told." His laugh boomed in the room while he ducked as though avoiding a well-deserved slap.

Lauren couldn't help grinning at his jab as she trailed him into the kitchen. Danger still hovered over her like a dark shadow, but she felt as though she'd found a temporary haven at the big man's house. At least for the moment.

Caleb flipped a burger on a flat griddle and pressed down with a spatula. Fragrant steam rose with a hiss, and Lauren's stomach rumbled an answer.

"We're about ready here," he told her. "How you coming on that salad?"

"Finished." She used the knife to slide chopped cucumber from the cutting board into a large bowl of salad greens and tomatoes. "I don't know why, but I'm surprised a man who lives alone eats salad."

He peeled the cellophane off of a slice of cheese. "First of all, I haven't spent a night alone in this house since the first day I moved in. There's always somebody who needs a good meal and a bed for the night." He slapped the cheese on a patty. "And second, just because I'm a man doesn't mean I shouldn't eat healthy."

Lauren decided not to comment on the questionable health benefits of greasy hamburgers, since the smell of them was about to drive her crazy.

A few moments later, he slid the burgers onto a platter. He lifted his head and called toward the living room. "Take a break, brother. Food's ready."

The speed with which Brent appeared testified to the fact that he was as hungry as she. Lauren smiled as she set the salad bowl on the counter beside the platter of hamburgers. The plates didn't match, and a couple of the fork handles were bent, but who cared? She was so hungry her knees felt wobbly.

A pan of hot pork and beans in one hand, Caleb opened the back door and spoke to the boys outside. "Anybody hungry?"

"I am."

"Yeah!"

Lauren stepped aside as Jake and Mush stampeded the kitchen.

"Whoa, hold up there. What are you forgetting?" Caleb's glare stopped them short.

"Oh, yeah."

They both returned to the table on the porch. Curious, Lauren glanced through the open door and saw them empty their pockets of cigarettes and lighters onto the table.

"I don't allow cigarettes in my house," Caleb explained.

When the guys returned, they stood near the food-laden counter, clasped their hands in front of them and bowed their heads.

Caleb looked at Brent. "Brother, you got a prayer in you tonight?"

Brent grinned. "Of course."

He stepped closer to Lauren, so close their arms almost touched. His nearness threatened to distract her, but she forced herself to listen as he prayed a blessing over the food.

When he said, "Amen," both young men echoed the word and then practically leaped for the stack of plates. Beneath their baggy clothes, Lauren realized they were both thin. When was their last meal? Caleb had called them crackheads in the car. So these two young men, who looked as if they shouldn't even be out of high school, were addicted to crack cocaine? A sad knot formed low in her throat. She didn't often pray during the day, but she found herself forming a mental prayer for these two boys as she filled her plate.

Had a hamburger ever tasted so good? Melted cheese

dripped onto her finger, and she licked it off without a single care for manners.

Jake and Mush didn't appear to be concerned about manners, either. They took huge bites of their burgers and forked beans into their mouths without a second's pause.

"Slow down, you two." Caleb frowned across the table at them. "The way you're tackling that food you'd think you haven't eaten in days. I know for a fact you had a good breakfast this morning, because I fed it to you."

Mush, the one with the lip stud, gave him a scowl. "Pop-Tarts don't count as a good breakfast."

"Hey!" Caleb drew himself up. "Pop-Tarts are good food. I eat them. And don't talk with your mouth full."

Lauren hid a smile. Healthy meals, he'd said? She forced herself to slow down lest Caleb point out her lack of manners, too.

Beside her, Brent stabbed a forkful of salad and spoke in a conversational voice. "So, are you two originally from Vegas?"

"Not me," Jake answered around a mouthful of burger. He glanced at Caleb, swallowed, and then went on. "I came up here a couple of months ago from Yuma. Got a buddy who's gonna get me a job at a gas station soon."

Lauren glanced at Caleb, whose mouth pressed into a thin line. Apparently he'd heard that before.

"I've been here my whole life." Mush scraped the last of the beans off his plate. "But when my dad gets out of jail, he and I are gonna take off, maybe go to California or Florida."

"Not a bad idea to put some distance between yourself and your old ways," Caleb commented as he left his chair with an empty plate and headed toward the counter for a second helping of salad.

"That's what Dad says." Mush held the last bite of burger between two fingers in front of his lips. "But mostly he says he wants to get as far away from that a—" His lips snapped shut on the word, and he flashed a guilty glance at Lauren. "From Gaines and his homies as he can." He popped the burger into his mouth.

At the mention of the detective's name, Lauren's fork froze halfway from her plate to her mouth. Beside her, Brent jerked upright in the hard chair.

"Are you talking about Detective Gaines from the Las Vegas police?"

How Brent managed to maintain a calm tone as he asked the question, Lauren didn't know. Her hands were trembling so badly her fork rattled against her plate when she set it down. She hid them under the table.

Both boys nodded, chewing. Mush gulped, then answered in a voice full of scorn. "He's a jerk and a crook. Nailed my pop for possession when he didn't have anything on him, not even a joint. Said some jail time would teach him a lesson." He shook his head and called the detective a name under his breath that might have earned him a slap from Caleb if he'd heard.

Lauren's gaze locked onto Brent. Could Gaines really be a crooked cop? Or was Mush merely bitter about the police officer who arrested his father?

Appetite gone, she pushed her half-full plate away. If it was true, why was Gaines trying to frame her for murder?

SEVENTEEN

Because he was seated beside her, Brent noted Lauren's trembling hands clenched in her lap. He forced himself to go ahead and take the bite of salad on his fork, chew and swallow, as though he hadn't just learned a piece of shocking news about the detective who was no doubt looking for them at this very moment.

First I need to know if there's any truth to the kid's accusation.

He stabbed at a chunk of tomato and forced his voice into nonchalance. "So is this Gaines guy really crooked, or is he just a jerk?"

"He's crooked as a bent nail," Jake answered. "Everybody knows that." Mush nodded with vigor.

Caleb returned to the table with a second loaded plate. Brent didn't speak but gave him a questioning look.

The big man shrugged. "That's the word on the street."

Lord, this is big. But what does it mean to us?

Facts ticked through his mind. Gaines had interrogated Lauren using a method intended to force a confession from a guilty suspect. He'd refused to consider the possibility that Lauren's international travel could have a legitimate reason. Then there had been that ludicrous suggestion of a connection between Lauren and Frank because they'd both been in Costa Rica, even though they weren't there at the same time. Would an honest police detective question those things? Possibly. But how could Brent factor in his instinct, the gut feeling that there was something not quite right about Gaines's certainty that Lauren was guilty?

And what about that envelope he'd seen pass between Gaines and the other man, the one who'd attended their workshop session?

"You guys seem to know stuff about this town. Let me ask you a question." He calmed his features and let his gaze bounce from Jake to Mush. "Do you know Gaines's buddies, the ones he works with?"

Mush shoved a bite into his mouth, and Jake shrugged. Across the table, Caleb gave Brent a shrewd, narrow-eyed glance but didn't speak.

"For instance," Brent went on, "there's this guy, kind of short and thin, blondish hair. Clean-cut. Narrow face. Does that sound like anybody you know? Maybe an undercover cop who works with Gaines?"

"I've met some undercover cops," Jake answered, "but they don't look like that."

An uncertain expression crossed Mush's face. "Maybe. I'm not sure."

"Wait. I have a picture." Lauren jumped up from the table and disappeared in the direction of the hallway. She returned moments later, tapping the screen of her cell phone.

"Here he is." She handed the phone to Mush. "Do you recognize him?"

The young man studied the screen. Brent saw the

moment he recognized the man in the photo. His lips parted, and his eyes went round.

"Yeah, I know that guy." He shoved the phone back toward Lauren as if it had burned him.

"Is he a dirty cop?" Brent asked.

"He ain't no cop." Mush put his fork on his empty plate and tossed his crumpled napkin on top. "He's a, what-do-you-call-'em? A guy who dresses up like famous people."

Caleb supplied the word. "A celebrity impersonator."

Disappointment stabbed at Brent. The Hollywood Casino was full of celebrity impersonators. This man was probably one of Gaines's stooges, on his payroll to spy on Brent and Lauren during the workshop. That information wasn't going to help them solve anything.

"Yeah, that's right." Mush shook his head. "But that ain't his real job. You don't want to mess with that guy."

Brent's ears pricked to attention again. "Why not?"

Mush put an arm on the table and leaned forward. "He's a collector, dude. Name's Jarrell. He's Cicalo."

Brent had no idea what that meant, but the caution in Mush's tone, the way he lowered his voice when he spoke the word, told him it wasn't good.

Caleb broke the moment by leaning back in his chair and tossing his fork on his plate. "Man, if I eat any more I'm going to hurt myself. That was a good salad, Lauren. I can feel those vegetables making me healthy already."

The caution in the look he gave Brent warned him to drop the subject.

With a visible effort, Lauren shook off her tension and replied without a tremor in her voice. "I'm not sure the salad could offset the grease in the hamburger, but it tasted so good it was worth it. Thank you, Caleb. To show my appreciation, I'll do the dishes."

She half rose from her chair, but Caleb stopped her. "No way. We've got rules around here. You eat, you work." He leveled a stern look on Mush and Jake, who immediately rose and started clearing the table.

While the boys washed up, Brent remained at the table with Lauren and Caleb. They exchanged tense, silent glances, but Caleb's heavy scowl warned them not to mention Gaines or the mystery *collector* again. Brent clamped his jaw shut, his tension mounting, until the dishes were cleaned and put away.

"Good job. Thank you." Caleb rose and approached the back door. "Now, scram. Come back in the morning if you're not too good for a Pop-Tart."

"Thanks, Preacher Man." Mush held a fist toward Caleb, who tapped his knuckles with his own.

Jake nodded farewell in Brent and Lauren's direction, and also knocked knuckles with Caleb on his way out. "See you."

Caleb closed the door behind them. He stood with his back toward Brent and watched through the blinds for a moment. A heavy silence filled the kitchen. When Brent saw the boys' figures pass by the kitchen window on their way out of the yard, Caleb closed the blinds and twisted the dead bolt. Then he turned toward the table, his expression solemn.

"If you two are mixed up with the Cicalo gang, you're in a whole lot more trouble than I thought. They're brutal."

A brutal gang? The hamburger turned to cement in Brent's insides.

* * *

Questions whirled in Lauren's brain, but she couldn't squeak any words through a mouth that had gone completely dry. One look at the worried expression on Caleb's face, and she wasn't sure she wanted to know the answers anyway.

Brent's fingers pressed white against the edge of the table. "Who are the Cicalo gang?"

"Mafia."

The word sliced through the room. Lauren's head went light, and faint buzzing began in her ears.

Caleb returned to his chair at the table, turned it around and sat backward on it with his arms resting across the top. "I don't know much about them, only what I've picked up here and there. They're out of Chicago, but they have a strong presence in Vegas. Most of the Mafia organizations do. Word has it they've got fingers in just about everything—drugs, prostitution, illegal gambling, you name it."

Lauren found her voice. "I thought prostitution and gambling were legal in Nevada."

"They are, and they're strictly regulated. But there are a million and one ways to circumvent the laws and avoid paying the taxes."

"What's a collector?" Brent asked.

"That's the guy who comes to collect what you owe when you lose an illegal bet. They're usually big, and always mean and ruthless." His arms dropped over the chair back and his hands grasped to form one big fist. "I actually had a couple of job offers when I first moved here, before my reputation as a Christian spread."

Lauren could see why. If a guy as big and muscular as Caleb came knocking on her door, she'd scramble to pay whatever she owed in record time.

"That doesn't sound like this man at all." She raised her cell phone to indicate the photo. "He's on the small side."

"Yeah." Brent eyed the size of Caleb's shoulders. "You make two of him, maybe three."

"Collectors don't *have* to be muscle-bound. It just helps. If you're ruthless enough, word spreads and all you have to do is ask nicely. People will throw money at you to keep you happy."

Fear squeezed her throat. She remembered his calm glance when their eyes met during the workshop. "So this Jarrell guy is ruthless?"

Caleb's hands splayed open for a moment. "I have no idea. I've never heard of him. But if he's in bed with the Cicalos, like Mush said, I believe it."

One piece of the puzzle snapped into place. Lauren placed a hand on Brent's arm. She tilted her head toward the back bedroom where she'd taken the bag of money.

"Frank was paying a gambling debt," he said quietly, "and Jarrell was coming to collect the money."

Frank, an illegal gambler. She didn't find that hard to believe at all. Though he'd never said anything to her that hinted of a tendency to break the law, Frank's language had been offensive and his reputation of being a rowdy and frequent drinker was no secret. A technical genius, but not someone she would have ever chosen to spend her free time with.

"That fits." She weighed the scenario in her mind. Frank knew he was coming to Las Vegas for this conference months ago. He'd told her about it her first week of work and then also told her she'd have to take her predecessor's place in copresenting the workshop with him. So he decided to place a bet, or maybe a few bets, with an illegal gambling ring in Vegas. There were certainly ways to place illegal bets in Atlanta, but maybe the stakes were higher in Las Vegas. Then when he lost, he brought cash to settle his bet.

Something about it still didn't feel right.

Apparently Brent agreed. "But why would he ship the money to your attention?" he asked.

She was at a loss to explain. "I have no idea."

"Ship money?" Caleb stared at Brent for a moment. His gaze switched to Lauren and then to the short hallway leading to his bedroom. "There's money in that bag?"

There's nothing slow about this guy.

"Are you sure you want to know?" Brent asked. "It might be best if you didn't."

He leaned back and folded his arms across his chest. "I probably don't, brother. But if I've got Cicalo money in my house, I think somebody had better tell me what's going on."

She exchanged a glance with Brent. A wave of guilt washed over her. Caleb was a decent man, a Christian man. He spent his life helping people who desperately needed help. Could they drag him into a mess that could very well land him in jail? Or maybe worse, since the Cicalo's reputation was so violent?

On the other hand, did they have a choice? Apparently some very nasty people were after her, and since Brent had run away with her, probably him, too. Fear shuddered down her spine at the thought of being caught by a crooked cop, or worse, a Mafia gang.

Brent watched her closely, waiting for her agreement to tell Caleb the details of their situation. They needed his help. If they didn't figure out what was going on fast, they might all end up dead like Frank. She nodded.

Brent laid his arms on the table's scratched surface and began.

EIGHTEEN

Brent stared at Caleb's monster of a computer monitor and watched as a gigantic list of codes scrolled across the screen. The main servers at Sterling Foods' Atlanta headquarters had been working for hours to decipher Frank's encryption code. Impossible to tell if the program was making any headway or not. A call to the corporate attorney had proved frustrating. His cell phone was turned off, and as yet, he hadn't returned the call. Since it was close to ten o'clock back in Atlanta, Brent wasn't sure he'd even get the message before morning.

His call to Mason had been almost as frustrating. Caleb had been far more understanding when Brent detailed their situation. Mason nearly exploded.

"Are you insane?" The P.I.'s voice had carried from the little phone speaker all the way across the room. "Everybody's heard of the Cicalo family. What has this woman gotten you into, Brent?"

Even though he'd held the phone to his ear, the words were apparently discernable to the others. Lauren's face had blanched, and Caleb had held a hand out for Brent's phone.

"Let me handle him while you get back to work," he had said.

Brent had gladly turned Mason over to Caleb and returned to the computer.

He stared at the scrolling codes. Not that he could do anything except watch the program do its work.

Lauren appeared behind him with two steaming mugs. She handed him one and leaned against the back of one of the padded living-room chairs nearby.

"Chamomile tea." She brought her mug to her lips and sipped. "Apparently it soothes your stomach when you're detoxing from drugs. Caleb says it will help keep us calm."

"A two-hundred-eighty-pound construction worker with a ponytail serves chamomile tea and Pop-Tarts to drug users, and makes them wash the dishes." He gave a soft laugh. "He's quite a guy."

Brent blew the steam away from the surface of his tea and took a cautious drink. The flavor was mild, the odor faintly floral. From one of the bedrooms down the short hallway, the low drum of Caleb's voice could be heard as he talked with Mason.

"How's it coming?" Lauren pointed toward the screen.

"Okay, I guess. It'll take time, that's all." He tilted back in the lopsided desk chair and propped his elbows on the arms, the hot mug in his hands. "I've been wondering about something. Your ex-boyfriend."

Spots of color appeared high on her cheeks. "I'd prefer to refer to him as my ex-boss."

For some unknown reason, her words pleased him. He hated to think she harbored feelings for a prior relationship. "Okay, but I'm wondering how he fits into all this."

She shook her head, clearly confused. "What makes you think he's involved?"

"Because him showing up in our workshop today is too weird not to at least consider."

"Well, he *is* involved in the computer industry and this is one of the biggest technical conferences in the nation." She raised a finger to forestall his argument. "No, he didn't have to attend our session, but I have a feeling he did that to intimidate me. That's exactly the kind of thing he does."

Her explanation made sense, but he heard a note of hesitation in her voice. "You said he was involved in unethical business practices, right? Well, apparently Frank was, too. Don't you find that strange?"

Lines appeared in her forehead. "David didn't gamble, at least not that I knew of. The questionable practices involved unreported income from clients." Her expression grew grim. "Tax evasion."

"Didn't Caleb say that was exactly the reason for illegal gambling in a state where it's legal?"

She gave a hesitant nod. "But I never heard David mention Frank, or vice versa."

Maybe he was being overly suspicious, but he couldn't shake the idea that the two were somehow connected. What did they have in common? Maybe several things, but the most obvious was standing in front of him. "How did you learn about the job at Sterling Foods?"

"I saw an advertisement on a professional search website, and applied online. The recruiter called and talked to me on the phone first, then invited me in for an interview." She lifted the tea mug to her lips but spoke before she sipped. "That's when I interviewed with you. I had to lie to David and tell him I had a doctor's appointment, and I was taking off the whole afternoon."

An online applicant. Brent swiveled around in the chair and stared at the scrolling screen for a few seconds. Frank was the technical programmer in charge of supporting the company's online applicant system, which meant he'd had access to all the resumes they received. Could he have done something to give Lauren's application a higher priority, to bring it to the attention of the human-resources department? Yes, he could have, with a few keystrokes. But why?

Wait a minute. He turned back toward Lauren. "Earlier you told me David questioned you if you took too long at the grocery store. He didn't say anything about you taking half a day for a doctor's appointment?"

"No, but—" She stopped, and her expression became doubtful. "No, he didn't. I wonder why."

Caleb strode into the room and handed Brent his cell phone. "Mason's good with everything. He's going to see what he can dig up about this Jarrell character for us. Have you gotten anything yet?" He pointed at the computer monitor.

Brent and Lauren continued to stare at each other. After a moment, Brent looked away. Something wasn't right about the whole David-Frank thing, but he couldn't put his finger on it. He'd think more about it later, but best stick to one thing at a time.

He swiveled back around in his seat, but his reply that he'd made no progress yet died on his lips. The program had stopped. Frank's encryption code was displayed on the screen.

"I found something."

Excitement tickled the base of his skull as he highlighted the code and copied it onto the computer's clipboard. No wonder he hadn't been able to come up with it on his own. The code was an entirely random string of numbers and letters—the hardest code to decipher, as Frank obviously knew.

He closed out that window and opened another one, this time accessing the most recent of Frank's Las Vegas files. At the prompt for the encryption code, he pasted the contents of the clipboard and then clicked the submit button.

A database opened. Columns of data appeared on the monitor. The first few were immediately recognizable as names and addresses, and the state abbreviations were from all over the U.S. Then came an alphanumeric code—another code!—followed by a formula. The last column was a number.

Lauren and Caleb drew close to hover behind him and examine the data over his shoulders.

"What does it mean?" Caleb asked.

A new line appeared at the top of the screen, and a few seconds later, another one.

"It's a database," Brent said, watching in fascination as the data expanded before their eyes. "And it's updating while we watch."

"A real-time IP network application." Lauren's voice held a grudging note of admiration. "Just like you and I demonstrated today. Frank's specialty."

"That doesn't answer my question." Caleb stabbed a finger at the screen, leaving a smudgy fingerprint over one of the columns. "Wait a minute. Those look like odds for a bet."

Brent's pulse kicked up, and blood surged faster through his veins. Two dash one. Eight dash three. That formula did look like odds. And the number in the last column might be a dollar amount. But some of them were really big numbers. "Hold on. If we're getting real-time updates, somewhere there's a program that feeds information into this database."

He pressed a series of keys, and the program file opened. His eyes scanned the code until he found what he was looking for—the source of the constantly updating data. In a separate window he opened the internet and keyed in a website address.

"WWW.Skorzbiz.com?" Lauren laid a hand on his shoulder and leaned closer to the monitor. "What is that?"

With an effort, Brent ignored the sensations her contact stirred up. "If I'm not mistaken, Skorz means scores, as in sports scores."

The website opened. A banner flashed dollar signs in the corners, and giant letters proclaimed Bet on the Big Game! Win Big Money!

"It's an online betting website," Caleb said.

"That's right." Brent switched back to the program code. "And if the right passcode is entered in the ID field, the user is taken to a series of private pages that are not accessible to the general internet." He turned the chair sideways and looked at them. "They are hosted, along with this database, in a protected area of Sterling Foods' corporate computer system."

"Wow." Lauren stepped back to lean against the padded chair. "Frank was running an illegal gambling ring on our company's system."

"Not just Frank," Caleb corrected. The big man's expression sent a chill marching across Brent's arms. "But the Cicalo Mafia family."

NINETEEN

While Brent kept examining Frank's program code, Lauren returned to the kitchen with her empty tea mug. Brent's questions about David plagued her. Why hadn't David pressed her for details about that four-hour doctor's appointment? She'd been delayed in traffic for fifteen minutes once, and he'd almost gone ballistic.

"I found another table in the database." Brent's voice held unsuppressed excitement. "This one records whether the bet was a win or a loss. There's also another code. I think it's supposed to identify the name of the collector, but I can't see a translation anywhere. If I'm right, there are a bunch of collectors."

Lauren ran clean water from the faucet into the mug and swirled it around. They were uncovering some important evidence, no doubt about that, but what could they do with it? They certainly couldn't call Detective Gaines. From what Brent said, he was in as deeply as the deceptively plain-looking collector, Jarrell.

Her thoughts circled back to David. Was he somehow connected with all this? Earlier, when his malicious glare from the back row of the conference room had set her nerves on edge, she would have said yes without a second thought. But now, after she had time to consider the circumstances, she couldn't see how.

Brent's cell phone rang in the other room. She slung the water out of the mug and set it in the sink, then hurried to join the men.

Brent pressed a button and held the phone to his ear. "Yeah, Mason. What do you have?"

He fell silent, listening. Lauren exchanged a look with Caleb, then they both watched Brent's expression go from expectant to serious.

"That's what we heard, too." A pause, then he nodded. "You know it, buddy. Thanks for doing this, Mason. I'll add a couple of lobster tails to that filet, okay?"

With that mysterious parting, Brent disconnected the call. He faced them with a sober expression. "The collector's name is Boyd Jarrell. He's a female impersonator at the Hollywood Casino, but he also does private work, parties and so on. Plays a bunch of different celebrities. Celine, Cher, Reba." His fingers tightened on the arms of the black desk chair. "Mason called a contact who's familiar with the Cicalo gang and verified that he's a collector for their gambling division. And he's apparently not a very nice man if clients don't pay what they owe."

"A female impersonator." Caleb's gaze slid to her.

The blood drained from Lauren's face, leaving her cheeks damp and cold. That explained why the blackjack dealer had been so insistent that he knew her. Someone had actually dressed up as her, sat gambling beside Frank for hours in the casino, then followed him to his hotel room and shot him.

Was that why Boyd Jarrell had looked familiar? Was it the similarity to her own features she recognized in him? The light in the room dimmed, and a roar in her ears almost drowned out her thoughts. She wavered on unsteady legs.

Brent was out of his chair and beside her in an instant. She didn't resist as strong arms circled and supported her.

"It's going to be okay," his whisper promised. "We'll get to the bottom of this."

Grateful for his touch, she leaned against him and almost let the sobs simmering deep within her rise to the surface. But then she straightened. She didn't know why this was happening, but she didn't intend to stand around like a helpless female—a spoiled little girl, to quote Lisa—and let herself be framed for murder. She wanted answers, and she wanted them now.

She took a backward step, out of Brent's embrace, and announced, "I'm going to call David."

Lauren sat on the edge of the couch cushion, her cell phone clutched in her hand. David's name and number appeared on the screen, but her finger hesitated over the button that would connect the call. Part of her was afraid of what she would discover. Did David really betray her to a violent Mafia gang? And if he did, why? Was she so dependent on others to take care of her that she was clueless, gullible? An easy target for manipulation?

"Are you sure you want to do this?" Brent watched her from his seat in the worn chair to her right. "You don't have to, you know."

Of course she didn't have to. But then she'd never know the truth, would she?

Caleb, seated in the second chair, leaned forward, his arms on his knees. "Let's pray about it."

His words surprised her. Pray about what? She either made the call or she didn't. By the time she turned a curious glance his way, his eyes were closed and his head bowed.

"Lord, we need some guidance here. We need to understand how our sister got tangled up in this scheme, which clearly isn't Your plan for her."

Praying for guidance? Brent had said something similar earlier. She snuck a glance at her boss, who nodded in agreement with Caleb, his eyes also closed. These two took God's involvement in their lives to a whole different level, one that was alien to her.

Caleb's prayer continued. "So we're asking for wisdom on whether she should make this call. And if so, we're asking You to guide the conversation and tell us what we need to know. Amen." He raised his head and said to Lauren, "There."

As if that was supposed to do something. Was she supposed to see a sign flashing in her mind? An arrow maybe? If so, it didn't appear. And she didn't have time to wait for it. Either calling David was a good idea or a bad idea, but all she could do was what she thought best.

She decided to make the call.

Her watch read after eight o'clock. The last conference session would have ended a few hours ago, so hopefully his phone would be on.

The ringing stopped, and noise filled the line. The musical chimes of a dozen slot machines combined with the mumble of different voices.

"What have you done, Lauren?" David's loud words cut through the din. "The cops are looking everywhere for you."

"What have *I* done?" She allowed outrage to creep into her tone. "I'm calling to ask you the same thing."

"Hold on a minute. I can't hear a thing. I'm going up to my room so I can talk without being overheard." He sounded irritated.

Yeah, well so was she.

She heard the *ching-ching-ching* of a slot machine cashing out and listened until the distracting noise faded into the background. Her fingers tightened around the phone as she waited, her spine stiff, for him to speak again. Brent and Caleb's eyes were fixed on her.

The background noise of the casino disappeared completely. "There," David said. "I'm in the elevator. Sheesh, Lauren, did you really kill Frank Labetti?"

Her body went rigid. "Of course not. How could you even think that?"

"I don't know what to think. The cops are asking some pretty pointed questions about you."

"Did you tell them I'm deceptive and dishonest?" she snapped.

Brent left the chair and slid onto the cushion beside her to place a hand on her arm. "Stay calm."

She bit back a sharp retort and nodded instead. He was right. She wouldn't accomplish anything by arguing with David.

"David, I have to know. Are you involved with the mafia?"

"Are you?" he shot back.

She heaved a heavy sigh. So it was going to be that kind of conversation.

She schooled her voice. "Look, I know Frank Labetti was involved in an illegal gambling scheme, and for some reason he pulled me into it. Then he got himself killed." The breath she drew shuddered. "If I can't figure out what's going on, I'm afraid I might end up the same. Please, David. Help me."

"Hold on."

At the sound of resignation in his voice, Lauren's spirits rose a fraction. She heard the ding of an elevator, and nothing but David's breath for a long thirty seconds, followed by a door closing.

"There. I'm in my room. All right, I'll tell you what I know. I was at work one day and I got a phone call from a guy I know." A pause. "It's a guy I owe some money to. A lot of money."

"Gambling debts?" she guessed.

"Yeah." Embarrassment colored his tone. "If only the University of Kentucky had taken the NCAA title, I would have been in the black."

Lauren's spine lost a touch of its rigidity. That made sense, in a way. She'd never known David to gamble, but he was a sports fanatic in every sense of the word.

"Anyway," he continued, "this guy calls and tells me you've applied for a job at another company, and he wants me to let you go without a fuss. That hurt, Lauren. You kept it from me, and I thought we had a relationship going."

She blocked a stab of guilt at the pain in his tone. They'd had this conversation before, the day she left his company. He was a controlling, manipulative man, and she had been right to get away from him.

To pull him out of his pity party, she asked a question. "Why did they want me to leave Reynolds Sof-Tech?"

"They didn't. They wanted you at Sterling Foods, because they've got something going on there. I was supposed to give you a great reference if they called, and a bad one to anyone else to discourage them from hiring you. My guy told me they needed you at Sterling Foods because if someone who knew about technical stuff got that position, there was a risk they'd be exposed."

Her brain absorbed the meaning of his words. She sank against the back of couch. "You mean they wanted me for the Sterling Foods job because I have no technical ability? Because I'm unskilled?"

Her gaze sought Brent's. Was that why he'd given the okay to hire her? He shook his head *no,* his expression perplexed.

"That's right," David said. "I didn't want to lose you, Lauren, but I didn't have a choice. These people get what they want, one way or another."

Reeling from the revelation, Lauren managed another question. "Then why did you glare at me through that workshop this afternoon? Why did you attend at all?"

"Because I wanted to see you." He adopted the soft, wheedling tone she remembered so well. "I miss you, baby. When I saw you with that vice president, saw the way you were looking at him, I couldn't handle it. I got angry. He's your boss, right? Just like I was your boss."

The insinuation stung. Especially since she'd been fighting off romantic thoughts of Brent all day.

In the background on David's end came a knocking sound.

"Hold on. There's somebody at the door. I can't stand those geeks who try to organize these late-night conference parties. Let me get rid..." His voice faded. "What are you doing here?"

Lauren was confused. Was he talking to her or to the

person at the door? His question was spoken directly into the phone.

"What are you talking about?"

She heard the sound of a door being opened.

David's voice became slightly more distant, as if he'd lowered the phone from his mouth. "I'm glad you decided to come. Who needs the phone when we can talk in per—" He stopped mid-word. "Wait a minute. You're not Lauren."

Horror bloomed in an instant. If David thought *she* was at the door, then it had to be an impostor.

Jarrell.

She shot to her feet and shouted, "Don't let him in."

A noise came through the phone, both familiar and unknown. A muffled *crack crack*. In an instant she identified the sound. She'd only heard it on television shows, never in person. The sound of a gun with a silencer being fired.

"David!"

The only answer to her scream was a hideous gurgle. Just like the one she'd heard through the door from Frank's room last night.

TWENTY

Brent knelt on the floor in front of Lauren, her cold hands sandwiched between his. She'd been exhibiting signs of shock for the past twenty minutes.

"He's dead." She shook her head, her gaze unfocused. "I can't believe David is dead."

"We don't know that," Brent said quietly, though a dreadful certainty in his gut said otherwise. "Maybe he's only injured. I'm sure the police have the casino staked out looking for us, so they probably had someone in his room within minutes after we called 9-1-1." He hoped the call from Caleb's cheap, prepaid phone couldn't be traced, but what could they do? If a man had been shot, they had to get help to him somehow.

Lauren didn't answer, only continued to stare, her expression tortured.

Caleb returned to the room with another steaming mug of tea, which he placed in front of her. "Drink this, sister. It'll make you feel better."

Lauren didn't move to pick it up. Instead, her gaze focused on Brent.

"Why did you hire me?"

Her words on the phone came back to him. Something about being unskilled, which made no sense. "We hired you because you were the best candidate for the job."

"Really? Because David said the Cicalo gang wanted me to get that job because I don't have technical skills. They didn't want me to discover Frank's database hidden on Sterling Foods' servers."

Brent raked his fingers through his hair, thinking. When he'd met with Lauren, he'd been given a folder with notes from the previous interviewers. Frank had been one of them, he did remember that, and that made sense. Lauren's job was to act as business liaison between Frank, the technical person and the nontechnical employees who used the systems Frank supported. The man who'd held the position before Lauren had possessed very little technical ability also, though he'd performed well enough to get a promotion that left his job open.

Brent remembered that the other interviewer, Lauren's manager who reported to Brent, had given her the thumbs-up. And there'd been something else in that file. A computer printout analyzing her skills and experience, and identifying her as the most qualified candidate. The printout had come from a program Frank supported.

"You were qualified for the job, Lauren." He squeezed her cold hands. "I was impressed by your answers to my questions during our interview, and by the way you handled yourself with professionalism. I approved hiring you based on that. A business analyst's number one responsibility is to communicate with nontechnical people, and that's one of your strengths."

He hesitated. How to say this without upsetting her? "But long before we scheduled your interview, the computer picked your resume from among all the others and identified you as a top candidate. Since Frank was the expert on that system, it's possible he rigged the results in order to move your application up to the top of the list."

She absorbed that information and then nodded. "So, Frank was watching the resumes that came in, looking for someone he thought he could hide his illegal activities from. When mine came in, he decided I was the one."

"That makes sense. No doubt he saw Reynolds SofTech on your application as your current employer. Since he was responsible for maintaining the database for the Cicalos, he probably knew David was one of their customers. That's what drew his attention to you in the first place."

Caleb, who had returned to his chair, broke into the conversation. "So where does that money in my bedroom come in?"

Lauren shrugged. "David didn't mention the money."

"Did he say anything about Frank, like why the Cicalo people killed him?" Brent asked.

She shook her head. "We didn't get that far in the conversation before…" She swallowed.

So they still didn't know what was going on. Brent sank back on his haunches. They didn't have any real proof of Lauren's innocence.

When his cell phone rang, he snatched it off the table and examined the screen. Mason.

He answered the call. "Please tell me you dug up something helpful."

"Man, it's good to hear your voice. Is Caleb with you?"

Why did Mason sound so relieved? "It's good to hear your voice, too, buddy. Yeah, he's right here."

"Whew. I know we just talked an hour ago, and I know you both say this woman is on the up-and-up, but when I saw the news I got this crazy idea maybe something had changed and she really had done you both in."

Brent pulled the phone back to give it a confused glance. "What are you talking about? What news?"

"You're not watching the news on television?"

"No." Brent stabbed a finger in the direction of the clunky old TV set and asked Caleb, "Does that thing work?"

"Yeah, sure." He jumped up and snatched the remote control from a side table.

On the other end of the phone, Mason continued. "I've been watching the Las Vegas news channel on the internet, and a few minutes ago a new story was posted. It's about your girlfriend."

Brent opened his mouth to correct Mason—Lauren was not his girlfriend—but the words died on his lips when the TV sprang to life. A blue banner with white letters across the bottom of the screen announced *Breaking News.* Above it, a female reporter with a microphone stood in front of a familiar sight, the entrance to the Hollywood Casino. She spoke directly into the camera.

"…A little over twenty minutes ago, when a 9-1-1 operator received an anonymous tip that a man had been shot at the Hollywood Hotel and Casino on Las Vegas Boulevard. That victim's identity has not yet been released, but we have received verification that his body was found in a room inside the Hollywood. Though there has been no official statement yet, the Las Vegas Police Department issued an All Points Bulletin for the arrest of twenty-four-year-old Lauren Elizabeth Bradley just moments ago."

On the couch, Lauren gasped. Brent grabbed her hand, and she squeezed his like a vice. Standing near the television set, Caleb's lips moved in a silent prayer.

The reporter continued. "At the same time, they released a missing person alert for Brent Emerson, a thirty-two-year-old executive from Atlanta. An unofficial source inside the LVPD informed us that Emerson is involved romantically with Bradley, and the police fear for his safety."

"What?" He reeled backward, as though from the impact of a blow.

Mason spoke in his ear. "I heard that. That's what it said on the internet, too."

The scene on the screen changed to a news station, and a reporter told the viewing audience, "We'll keep you posted on this breaking story as it develops. In other news tonight, a—"

Caleb pressed a button on the remote and muted the volume.

"I can't believe this," Lauren whispered, her voice husky. "Frank is dead. David is dead. And they think I'm going to kill you, too."

Brent's thoughts whirled. Things were moving too fast to keep up with. The pieces of information they'd uncovered all made sense, but they didn't have enough of them to paint a clear picture.

He spoke into the phone. "I'll call you back, Mason." Without waiting for a response, he disconnected the call. "We have to keep a clear head," he told Caleb and Lauren. "We can figure this out, we just need to work together."

Lauren shook her head with a jerk. "No. We can't

do this on our own anymore. The pit I'm in is getting deeper and deeper. We need to contact the police and tell them everything we know."

"I'm sure there are a lot of conscientious officers on the Las Vegas Police Department, but we know at least one of them who isn't," Brent said. "How can we be certain we're not just turning ourselves into another pawn of the Cicalos?"

He directed his question toward Caleb, who shook his head. "Don't ask me. My path doesn't cross with the police very often. I just hear people talk, and the people who talk to me don't have anything nice to say about the cops."

"The FBI, then," Lauren said. "Two people have been killed, and we have a bag full of money that belongs to the Mafia. Surely they'd be interested in hearing from us."

"How do we know who to contact within the FBI?" Brent didn't like to say it, but at this point his suspicions were on alert. If the Cicalo gang had corrupted a Las Vegas detective, how far did their reach extend?

He saw his fear mirrored in Lauren's expression. He also saw a wild look in her eyes, as though a full-fledged panic attack lurked nearby.

He looked at Caleb. "What do you think we ought to do?"

The man's answer came immediately. "Ask God for guidance."

Of course. That should have been Brent's first act.

Lauren leaped off the couch and stomped to the middle of the room. "What is it with you two? Can't you make a decision on your own?" Anger gave her voice volume. "I know you're both Christians, but so am I. God gave us brains for a reason. He wants us to use them." Her eyes flashed from Caleb to Brent.

The vehemence of her anger surprised him. Earlier, in the parking garage, she'd told him she believed *God helps those who help themselves.* Fine. Many people felt that way. But in this case, his brains weren't coming up with an answer on their own.

Caleb's gentle voice fell like rain on a raging fire. "God did give us brains, sister. But He also gave us a Spirit to guide us."

She whirled to glare in his direction but didn't say anything. The only part of her that moved was her trembling jaw. Tears sparkled in the eyes she turned on Brent. "I thought you said you wanted to help me."

He replied instantly. "I do. Lauren, I prayed for guidance earlier, when I didn't know whether to believe you or not, and I think the Lord wanted me to trust in your innocence. I wish I was hearing a firm direction right now, but I'm not. Still, something is telling me to wait." He glanced at his watch. After nine o'clock. "Look, we're in a safe place. We have some breathing space here. It's midnight back east. In eight hours the FBI office in Washington D.C. will open. We'll be able to call them and get directly in touch with whomever is in charge of cracking down on Mafia activity nationally." He rose and crossed the room to stand in front of her. "I really feel that we should wait until then."

He forced her to hold his gaze, to see how strongly he felt about this decision. Behind her tears, he saw fear in the green eyes, and his heart twisted in his rib cage. His arms itched to gather her in an embrace. He ached to whisper in her ear that he would protect her, that he would die before he let anything happen to her.

But then she blinked away the tears and jerked her face away from him.

"Fine. Do whatever you want. Whatever you feel *guided* to do."

Before he could stop her, she stormed out of the room. The sound of the bedroom door closing echoed down the hallway. Within seconds, another sound followed, the muffled sound of heartrending sobs.

Wordlessly, he looked at Caleb.

The big man shook his head. "Let her cry it out, brother. She can't hear anything clearly with all those emotions clogging her ears. The Lord will get through to her eventually."

With a sense of draining helplessness, Brent returned to his chair. He hoped so.

TWENTY-ONE

The words on the computer monitor wavered. Brent rocked back in the chair and rubbed his eyes with a thumb and forefinger. Over the past few hours his admiration for Frank's technical abilities had grown as he analyzed the entire program. It was a complicated system, with dozens of intricate calculations and no less than five layers of security. This database held enough information to blow the lid off of the Cicalos' illegal gambling ring and shut it down for good. But the data was also very clean. There were codes in use everywhere in order to conceal the identities of anyone within the Cicalo organization. Apparently Frank, or maybe his Cicalo bosses, didn't want to risk having their employees identified. The only names in the system were those of the gamblers who placed illegal bets through the internet, thousands of them. The amount of money that went through this system totaled in the millions.

Still, in the hands of the FBI, this information could probably incriminate a bunch of Mafia bad guys. Combined with other resources they no doubt possessed, maybe they could identify the people involved and put them away for a long, long time.

A loud snore vibrated down the hall from the second bedroom. A laugh huffed through Brent's lips. Caleb. He'd nodded off in the chair watching Brent work, until an hour ago when he announced he was calling it a night and stumbled sleepily down the hall.

Not a bad idea. I'm not covering any new ground here.

Tomorrow promised to be an eventful day, though hopefully not as eventful as the one just past. They all needed to get some rest so they could face it with clear heads.

He shut down the computer, flipped the living-room light switch and made his way down the hallway. The door on his left formed a forbidding barrier behind which Lauren slept. At least, he hoped she'd fallen asleep. He placed an ear against the wood and heard nothing but silence from the other side.

The sound of her wrenching sobs earlier had just about torn him apart. It had been all he could do not to break though that door and gather her in his arms to hold her while the emotional storm ran its course.

His sister's voice spoke clearly in his mind. *Charging in on your white horse again, eh, Knight-in-Shining-Armor?* He couldn't stop a grin at the memory of the sassy tone she always used on him.

Was that what he was doing, reacting to his own tendency to protect a damsel in distress? Lauren's image loomed in his mind's eye, so beautiful and sweet and, well, innocent. How could he not lend a hand to rescue someone charged with a crime she didn't commit?

Even as the thought crossed his mind, he knew he was lying to himself. Yes, it might have started that way, offering help to someone falsely accused. But the catch in his chest when he thought of Lauren, the longing to hold her and comfort her, the way she invaded every thought—all those things proved that sometime during the horror of the day, something wonderful had happened. He'd fallen in love with her.

Oh, Lord, what have I done? I can't fall in love with someone who works for me. I'll lose my job, and she'll lose hers.

A laugh at the ridiculous thought forced its way from his lungs. They had run afoul of a vicious Mafia gang and a crooked cop, and he was worried about losing his job?

Show us how to get out of this mess, God. I'll worry about the job later, when I'm sure we're not going to both end up dead.

He placed a palm flat against the door and whispered a prayer for her safety, then headed for the room he was to share with Caleb for what was left of the night.

Lauren lay across the top of the bedspread in the darkness, listening to Caleb snore. Her violent tears had cried themselves out hours ago but their source, the deep, yawning fear that fed them, refused to leave. She couldn't bear to think about tomorrow, because so many of the outcomes she could envision ended badly. Which would be worse—to be caught by the crooked Detective Gaines or to fall into the hands of the Mafia? Or even to be apprehended by honest police officers who couldn't see past the tangle of fake evidence that identified her as a murderer?

Mingled with her fear was guilt. Those men sleeping across the hallway were good people who were trying to help her, and how had she responded? She'd shouted at them for their beliefs. She'd been furious with them for praying. What was the matter with her?

She rolled to the other side of the mattress, her gaze fixed on the cracks of cool moonlight filtering through the mini-blinds.

The whole thing about praying for guidance had rubbed sandpaper against a raw place in her soul. A reminder of her failure. Here she was, trying to learn how to stand on her own two feet, how *not* to rely on anyone else to decide the course of her life, and what had she done? She'd put herself in the hands of not just one strong, capable man, but two. Was she incapable of making a decision on her own?

The one big decision she'd made lately, the step of independence of which she'd been so proud, had ended in disaster. It turned out landing that job at Sterling Foods hadn't even been her decision. She had been manipulated the whole time, a clueless pawn without skills. And now David was dead because of her, just as surely as if she'd pulled the trigger that had taken his life. The knowledge made her cringe, and she tossed fitfully back to the other side of the bed.

What of Caleb and Brent? Would they, too, end up dead because of her? Caleb, the strong man with a soft heart for drug users and prostitutes, the ones most people would rather ignore. And Brent…

Her heart wrenched at the thought of him. She'd done it again, she knew that now. Fallen for her boss. But to compare the feelings she held for Brent with those of her relationship to David was like comparing a bowling ball with a ping-pong ball. The bowling ball was solid and heavy, but a ping-pong ball could be blown away with a breath.

I can't drag Brent any further into this mess. If anything happened to him because of me, I wouldn't be able to live with myself.

Her decision was made in an instant. The only reason Brent and Caleb were hesitant to call the FBI was because of her. They were being overly cautious for her sake, but they were letting caution override good sense. The FBI needed to be called, and waiting until morning wouldn't gain anything. Surely they had a national hotline or something. A twenty-four hour emergency line.

And once she was gone, Brent would be safe. The Cicalo gang would have no reason to bother him any further.

Moving as quietly as possible, Lauren rolled off the mattress and crept around the edge of the bed to the dresser. The bag of money lay on the floor where she'd put it, beside Caleb's tool belt. She slipped the strap over her shoulder and the weight dragged against her muscles. Her shoes and purse lay on the floor where she'd kicked them off. She picked them up and held them in her hand. Better go barefoot until she got outside or risk waking the men with the tapping of heels against the linoleum in the kitchen.

Caleb's snores grew louder when she edged the bedroom door open. Brent's slow, even breathing was barely discernable beneath the loud rumble. Lauren pulled the door closed behind her and crept down the hallway at a snail's pace, careful not to make a sound.

Only when she pulled the back door closed behind her did she allow herself to breathe. Glancing around the yard, she dropped her shoes and stepped into them. The moon shone brightly in the sky and illuminated the sandy backyard with cold, white light. The porch smelled faintly of stale cigarette smoke. A full ashtray sat in the center of the plastic table, a disposable lighter beside it.

Lauren dug in her purse and pulled out her cell phone. Would information have a listing of a national hotline number for the FBI? She hoped so. Brent's warning about corruption in local law enforcement weighed heavily on her mind. What if she placed a call to the FBI and got in touch with someone like Detective Gaines?

Though fear threatened to swallow her, that was a risk she'd have to take.

When she started to key in 4-1-1, a shuffling sound nearby seemed to split the silence like an alarm. She jumped nearly out of her skin, and then immediately saw the source. A cat had rounded the corner of the house and was rubbing against the peeling stucco.

If the noise from a cat was that audible in the silence, she might as well shout into a megaphone. She needed to put some distance between herself and the house.

And not only for that reason. When the FBI sent someone to get her, she needed to be as far from this house as she could. Images from their drive through the neighborhood surfaced in her mind, especially the rough-looking young men drinking beer a couple of streets from here. Why hadn't she grabbed Caleb's car keys off the dresser?

What am I thinking? She couldn't steal his car. And even if she could justify the theft in her mind, it was too late now. She couldn't risk going back in there and waking them. She'd just have to keep her eyes open and find someplace that looked safe to make her call. Surely there was a gas station or convenience store nearby.

Swallowing her fear, she scanned the surrounding area. Music and voices carried down the street from a house halfway up the block. She edged to the corner and looked. Lights illuminated every window, and the front door stood open. Two figures leaned against a car parked at the curb in front of the house, apparently talking. Somebody must be having a party. So she couldn't go that way.

Light showed in the windows of several of the homes up and down the street, but most were dark. Lauren's gaze fell on the residence across the street, one of the dark ones. The home of the two women she'd seen earlier. Caleb had said they were dancers and had been heading to work. That meant they worked at night. Their house would be empty.

Not far enough away, but maybe their backyard will be a good place to make my phone call.

With a cautious glance in each direction, Lauren clutched the duffel-bag strap and walked out of the shadows, heading across the street. Though her instincts were to run, she forced herself to maintain a normal pace. What had Brent said? *Act like you belong here.* If she were seen, she'd draw far less attention by walking than running. At least her slacks and blouse were dark.

By the time she reached her destination, her heart threatened to pound through her rib cage. She slipped into the shadows in the women's side yard and collapsed against the house. Gulping in huge draughts of air, she waited until her pulse returned to something resembling normal, then edged around back.

Unlike Caleb's, this porch had no awning. The twelve-by-twelve square of concrete held a couple of overflowing garbage cans and an old charcoal grill. A dilapidated half-full bag of charcoal lay on the cement beside the grill, its side split to let chunks of briquettes spill out. Nearby, an untidy pile of wooden slats that used to be a decorative bench had been kicked off the edge of the porch. The yard shared one feature in common with Caleb's—a complete lack of cover. Moonlight washed every bare inch of the weed-strewn sand.

At least my phone call won't be overheard here. She fished her cell phone out of her purse and then set it and the duffel bag on the ground. Step one, to call information and get the hotline number. What a shame the women who lived here didn't have chairs on their back porch.

A sound reached her ears. The smooth purr of a car engine coming down the street. Headlights slashed through the shadows and moved across the side of the house as the car approached. Lauren shrank against the rough stucco, waiting for the vehicle to pass. A second set of lights flashed across the building as another car followed the first. Maybe they were partygoers heading for the house down the street. Only the engine sounds didn't recede, as they would if the car had driven past. Instead, they went silent as the engine was cut off.

Had the women who lived here returned home? Stomach tight, Lauren edged around the corner of the house and bent double to creep forward until she could get a peek at the driveway. What she saw chilled the blood in her veins.

The women's driveway was empty, but Caleb's was not. A white Grand Am had parked behind his Toyota, and a dark sedan stopped along the curb out front. Two figures got out of each car. Moonlight gave her a clear view of the driver of the Grand Am, and she recognized him immediately. Revulsion twisted her insides. Detective Victor Gaines.

He gestured toward the two men who emerged from the second car, and each of them drew weapons. They advanced toward Caleb's front door, holding handguns straight out in front of them.

But it was the sight of the fourth person that sent a shiver down Lauren's spine. Nausea threatened to defeat her, and the bitter taste of acid burned the back of her throat.

A slight figure lagged behind Gaines and the others. White moonlight shone on shoulder-length honey blond hair and illuminated a familiar profile.

The fourth person was her.

TWENTY-TWO

A noise from the other room dragged Brent out of a deep, exhausted sleep. He lay in the dark room, his groggy mind trying to identify the sound, when another noise reached him. The sound of clothing rustling, and the soft squeak of a shoe.

Before he could react, a hard weight slammed into his chest and pressed him down into the mattress.

"If you move, you're dead."

Fear tingled along his nerve endings. He opened his eyes and saw the dark outline of a man hovering over him. He identified the weight as a knee planted in the middle of his chest, and a gun barrel hovered inches from his forehead. The faint odor of gun oil filled his nostrils. Though he didn't dare turn his head, he could see in his peripheral vision that Caleb was in a similar predicament.

Lauren! Oh, no. They've come to get her.

"What is going on here?" Caleb bellowed. "This is my home. You have no right to be here."

"Shut up or I'll shoot you just for getting on my nerves," the gunman snarled.

Then someone spoke from the doorway. "Where is the money, Mr. Emerson?"

Brent knew that arrogant voice. Gaines. These must be crooked cops, then, not the Cicalo. A dubious relief took him. Maybe he could bluff his way out.

"Detective, is that you? What's happening?"

A soft chuckle answered him. "Don't play innocent. It's too late for that. Now tell me what you've done with the money."

Brent's mind grasped. The money was in the other room, with Lauren. He strained to hear a noise from the room across the hallway but failed. A wild hope galloped over him. It was only a matter of seconds before they kicked in that door and found her. But they didn't have her yet. If she'd been awakened by the commotion, maybe seconds was all she'd needed. She could have escaped through the window.

"We put it someplace safe," he told the detective. "Let us go, and we'll tell you where it is."

The man on his chest threw his full weight on his knee, and fireworks of pain exploded in Brent's body. Air rushed from his lungs and left him gasping.

"We're not here to bargain with you," the man growled.

Gaines spoke again. "Bring them out here where we can see each other."

Still struggling to regain his breath, Brent found himself jerked off the mattress by his shirt and shoved into the hallway. Sharp pain told him the guy had probably broken a rib or two. A different kind of pain stabbed at him when he saw that the bedroom door across the hall stood open. As he was shoved past, he searched the room in a glance. It was empty. Lauren wasn't there.

If they've hurt her, I'll tear them apart with my bare hands.

In the living room, Gaines flipped on a lamp. A tidal wave of relief nearly knocked him off his feet when he saw Lauren standing in front of the window. She looked unharmed, thank goodness.

Then he looked again. That wasn't Lauren. The lips, which curled into a harsh smirk, were too thin, and the eyebrows too thick. Lauren's chin was far more delicate. Most of all, the scornful eyes that watched him were brown, not green. Nobody who really knew her would ever mistake this impostor for Lauren.

"Boyd Jarrell." The words left his lips with a snarl.

Caleb entered the room, his captor holding a gun at the base of his skull. His gaze locked onto Brent's, and he shook his head in a silent warning.

Too late. Brent gulped at his mistake. He'd just let Gaines and Jarrell know they'd discovered the connection between them. No bluffing now.

"I see you know my associate," Gaines said. "Good. We won't waste time with introductions."

He gestured toward the chairs, and the gunmen pushed Brent and Caleb toward them. Pain stabbed at his rib cage when Brent lowered himself onto the threadbare cushion. His captor took up a stance beside him. He and Caleb faced each other, each with a gun barrel pointed at their heads.

"What have you done with Lauren?" Brent snapped.

Surprise stole over Gaines's features. "I was about to ask you the same question."

Brent clamped his jaw shut. He'd done it again. Every time he opened his mouth he gave Gaines more information.

The detective looked toward the fake Lauren. "Take a look, would you? It's possible the money is here somewhere. Fifty thousand in cash can't be easy to hide in a place this small."

Jarrell's answer was a slight nod, and then he disappeared down the hallway.

The number staggered Brent. He'd been carrying around *fifty thousand dollars* all day in a canvas bag. No wonder it was so heavy.

"How'd you find us?" Caleb asked.

Brent wasn't sure if he really wanted to know the answer, or if he was simply trying to occupy the detective until Brent could pull himself together.

Gaines examined him through narrowed eyes. "Ah, Mr. Buchanan, also known as Preacher Man." His head moved as he scanned the crosses covering the wall. "I can see where the nickname comes from. Surely you're not gullible enough to believe your charity cases are loyal to you."

Understanding dawned on Caleb's face. "Mush."

"He contacted me a few hours ago." The detective allowed a cold smile. "I paid him fifty dollars and promised to put in a good word with the judge about his father. I'm sure the money has changed hands by now, and Mr. Mush is floating in crack heaven."

Caleb didn't respond, merely shook his head, sadness flooding his eyes.

The sound of Jarrell's search drifted down the hallway, drawers being opened, doors being shut. Brent's nerves stretched taut. Was Lauren hiding in a closet or under the bed? Maybe if Jarrell found the duffel bag before he found her, the money would distract them for a while. She might gain a few extra moments to escape out a back window. A desperate hope, but he had to cling to something or he'd go crazy.

One thing was for sure, he wasn't going to give

Gaines any more information than he already had. Maybe he could get the guy talking about himself, and that would take the focus off Brent, give him time to think.

"Why are you doing this, detective? You're a cop. Aren't you supposed to uphold the law?"

"Oh, I do. You can't believe how many worthless thugs and meth-heads I clear off the streets of this town." Gaines backed up to lean against the wall beside the television set. "But a man's got to plan ahead. Do you know how pitiful my retirement income from the police force will be? I can't live on that." He shrugged. "So I'm padding a little."

Jarrell returned to the room. "The money isn't here, and neither is the girl."

Brent's spine sagged. There was no way Jarrell could miss that duffel bag. That could only mean that Lauren had left before this crew arrived and had taken the bag with her.

Doubt crept into his thoughts. Had she deserted him and Caleb, left them on their own to deal with the consequences? Had he been duped? Was she the black widow Mason had accused her of being from the start?

He straightened. No, he couldn't believe that. Lauren didn't kill anyone, and she wouldn't betray him.

But where was she? And where was that money?

The living-room window in Caleb's house came on. Lauren could see light around the edges, and an occasional movement through the closed mini-blinds. How long she crouched in the dusty sand, cell phone clutched in her fist, her body pressed close to the stucco siding of the women's house, she didn't know. Brent and Caleb were facing who-knew-what at the hands of a crooked detective and a vicious Mafia gang member, and it was because of her. Indecision wrestled with an urgent need to *do something*. But what?

Finally she forced herself to retreat to the back-yard, where she collapsed on the dirty concrete slab and dropped her face into her hands. Breath shuddered into her lungs. Brent had put himself in danger to help her, and if she didn't hurry he would end up just like David.

A solution occurred to her. Daddy! He would tell her what to do. She had her fingers on the screen of her phone almost before the thought completed itself in her mind.

No, wait. Her finger hovered over the button that would connect the call. She was doing it again, calling Daddy to bail her out of hot water.

This is different. Brent's life is in danger. He needs help, and I don't know what to do.

But how could Daddy help? He was in Italy. The most he could do is give her advice. And what would he say? He'd tell her to call someone official. Like the FBI.

She cleared the screen and punched in the number for directory assistance. A canned female voice spoke in her ear.

"Please state the city and state of the listing you'd like to find."

Her mind blanked for a second. What did she say to get a national toll-free number? "Washington, D.C." It was worth a try.

"Washington, D.C.," the voice repeated. "For what listing?"

"The Federal Bureau of Investigation," Lauren said.

"Please hold while we retrieve the number."

Five heartbeats later, the sound on the line changed, and then a live operator asked, "Do you want the number for the administrative offices?"

"Do you have a listing for some sort of emergency hotline?" Nerves made Lauren's voice quiver.

"Hold one moment, please." The operator responded calmly, as if people called to get the FBI's hotline number every day.

Seconds later the computerized voice returned with a toll-free number. Lauren's brain scrambled to remember since she had nothing to write with. She disconnected the call and punched in the number.

Her call was connected and answered almost immediately by a cool, professional male voice. "Federal Bureau of Investigation, Agent Lawson speaking. Please be aware that this call is being recorded. How may I help you?"

Lauren's mind blanked. What should she say that would get them here as quickly as possible, and yet wouldn't make her sound like a lunatic?

"A man's been killed," she blurted. "No, two men. And my friend is in danger."

"Ma'am if this is an emergency you need to hang up and dial 9-1-1."

"No!" Lauren's shout echoed off the cement and rang in the air. She jerked a fearful glance toward the corner of the house. Had she been heard? With an effort, she continued in a lower voice. "We think the Mafia is involved."

"Ma'am, the FBI is an investigative and intelligence agency. We can help, but your local police have rapid response systems in place to—"

"You don't understand. I'm talking about the Cicalo gang. The *Mafia*."

Agent Lawson's voice remained calm. "Ma'am, I see your call is coming from a cell tower in Las Vegas. If you'll give me your exact location, I can contact the 9-1-1 dispatcher for you. Help will be there in minutes."

Alarm slammed into her. He could see where she was? And he was about to send the police here.

"N-no." She snapped her mouth closed until she could go on without stammering. "I've made a mistake. Nevermind. Thank you."

With a stab at her cell phone, she disconnected the call. Her trembling fingers lost their hold on the phone, and it fell from her grasp.

Had she just signed Brent's death warrant?

TWENTY-THREE

A fist connected with Brent's jaw, and exploding stars blinded him.

"Where is she?" Gaines's voice held an intense edge that hadn't been there before.

He's getting scared. If he loses fifty thousand dollars, his gangster bosses probably won't be forgiving.

The detective's face swam into focus as the spots receded from Brent's vision. Across the room, Caleb's hands clutched the worn arms of his chair, fury apparent on his flushed face. The goon beside him pressed a gun's barrel against his temple, a clear warning not to move.

Brent raised a hand and gingerly touched his jaw. "I told you, I don't know. That's the truth."

Gaines's arm cocked back, ready to deliver another blow, but paused when Jarrell uttered a filthy word.

"This is getting us nowhere."

Jarrell's glare was so unlike Lauren's sweet smile that Brent couldn't believe he'd ever mistaken the two of them, even for an instant.

"Call Fortelli. Tell him what's going on. They've got to drop a net over the city, fast."

Gaines's fist flattened, and he scrubbed his hand

over his mouth. Brent saw the struggle on his face and the moment he decided Jarrell was right. He slipped a cell phone from his belt and speed dialed a number.

"It's me. The girl's gone, and so is the money." An angry voice blasted through the phone, the words indistinguishable. The detective's eyes closed while he waited for the tirade to end. "She can't get far. Every cop in the city is on the lookout, and her picture's on the wire. We'll find her. In the meantime, we're going to continue as planned, okay?" Another pause, and his jaw clenched. "All right."

He snapped the phone closed and spoke to Jarrell. "He's making a call. Wants us to hold until we hear back."

"They don't trust you." A smirk twisted Jarrell's lips. "They're afraid you'll mess up something as simple as a hit."

"Shut up," Gaines snapped.

A hit. Brent didn't like the sound of that. Were they talking about killing him and Caleb? A glance at Caleb's solemn face revealed he wasn't the only one who thought so.

Lord, wherever Lauren is, guide her to safety. Get her out of this.

Every time he took more than a shallow breath, white hot pain pierced his side. At least one broken rib, maybe more. He forced his thoughts away from his own misery. Time enough to think about that later.

"Whose money is it, anyway?" He spoke more to fill the silence than anything.

Gaines pointed a finger at him. "You shut up, too."

"Was it Frank's, maybe?"

A sarcastic laugh blasted out of the detective's mouth. "That idiot? You've gotta be kidding. If only he'd done as he was told, he might still be alive. But he had to go and get too big for his britches."

Brent liked the way this was going. If he kept Gaines talking, he might learn something important. Of course, he and Caleb might not live long enough to use the information, but you never know.

"Frank was a lot of things," Brent said, "but he wasn't an idiot. He was one of the sharpest programmers I've ever known."

Jarrell answered from the corner where he stood. "He thought so, too. That was what did him in."

"I don't understand."

"He did some good work." Gaines leaned against the edge of Caleb's desk, his arms folded across his chest. "Put a computer system in place that made some important people very happy. And very rich. He hid that system right under your nose, Emerson. What do you think about that?"

The detective was talking about the online gambling website, and the secret database. He had no idea Brent had found that database using the computer six inches away from him. And Brent wasn't going to tell him.

"Be careful, Gaines," Jarrell spoke in a warning tone.

"What? These guys aren't going to be able to tell anybody anything."

So they were planning to kill them. Brent looked at Caleb and saw his lips moving in silent prayer.

Gaines crossed to stand in front of Brent's chair. Brent had to tilt his head back to look the guy in the face.

"Your squeaky-clean company has been running the biggest online gambling organization in the nation right under your nose. Labetti put everything in place, made a good name for himself. But he got cocky. Wanted a bigger role."

"So that money came from illegal gambling? Frank collected money from lost bets?"

A sarcastic laugh came from Jarrell. "That geek was no collector. He lacked the finesse the job requires."

Considering Jarrell's reputation for being a vicious collector, his comment sent a shiver marching across Brent's arms.

"Yeah, but he wanted to try," Gaines said, "and the bosses gave him a shot at it. Even sent him on a trip to set up one of the offshore accounts. Then they let him collect on a couple of Georgia bets, to give him a taste of the job. If only he'd done as he was told, it might have turned out okay for him. But instead of transferring the money like he was supposed to, he insisted on bringing it to the bosses in person. Said he wanted to talk with them."

Offshore accounts. Frank's Costa Rica trip, probably. Lauren had the bad luck of choosing a weekend escape to a Caribbean island that also happened to be known for money laundering.

"Even then, he might have been okay," Jarrell said. It was so strange, hearing his voice from a face that was made up to resemble Lauren's. Brent had a hard time looking at the guy. "But he started hinting around that he was indispensable, that nobody could access all that computer stuff except him, and they'd better keep him happy. That proved how stupid he was. You don't threaten the people who run this organization."

"If this organization—" they were carefully avoiding naming the Cicalos, so Brent did, too "—is as successful as you say, surely they have other people in Atlanta besides Frank. Why not take care of Frank back home? Why let him come all the way to Las Vegas to kill him?" Brent eyed Jarrell. "Just so you'd have the privilege of getting rid of him?"

"Actually, that decision had to do with timing. There are two hotshot computer jocks in Chicago who hacked into Labetti's system months ago. They've replicated his database and have been working the bugs out. This weekend they're going to flip the switch that takes control from Frank's system to the new one."

So Frank's doom had been sealed months ago. Maybe even before the Cicalo gang had arranged for Lauren to take the job at Sterling Foods. He tried to catch Caleb's eye, to see what he thought of this news, but the street preacher had his eyes squeezed shut, his lips moving silently at a rapid pace.

"Where does Lauren fit into all this?" Brent raised his hand to gesture vaguely, and the gunman at his side pressed the gun against his temple. His gaze slid to Jarrell. "And don't tell me she got dragged in so you could impersonate her, because you don't look anything like her."

Jarrell's painted smile spread across his face. "Ah, but looks can be deceptive. I make a living on that premise. From the moment Labetti pinpointed her as an unwitting partner, I've been studying her. I even took a trip to Atlanta dressed as her to buy a gun, and I filmed her for several days so I could perfect her gestures and her accent. I like to be thorough."

The thought of this creep stalking Lauren, recording her movements, stirred a powerful nausea in Brent's stomach.

Realization dawned. "Somebody set her up from the beginning. Frank unearthed her resume, but someone else gave him the approval to push for her to be hired. They intended to pin her for Frank's murder all along."

Jarrell's gaze slid to Gaines. "He's not stupid, I'll say that for him."

"Look, Emerson, the girl was just too easy." Gaines shook his head. "She had a connection with someone who owed us, and she had traveled to Costa Rica a few months before she applied for the job as Frank's partner. Plus, she had the same general build as Jarrell, here. A cut-and-dried setup. How could we resist?"

The words fell like blows on Brent's ears. *Oh, Lauren, baby, you never had a chance.*

Lauren sat on the cement, her back resting against the dancers' door, and stared at the silver-washed back-yard. She was out of ideas. Her call to the FBI had proven nearly fatal and might still end in Brent and Caleb's deaths before the night was over. If Agent Lawson was able to pinpoint her exact location, he might unwittingly send crooked cops. If not, Detective Gaines and Boyd Jarrell would certainly kill both men soon. And here she sat, fifty yards away, helpless to stop them.

So much for the brains God had given her.

Caleb's words came back to her, echoing in the empty spaces of her mind. *God did give us brains, sister. But He also gave us a Spirit to guide us.*

Sister. And Caleb also called Brent brother. She'd heard that term before. It was a way of acknowledging their shared faith, their belief in God.

But I don't have the faith you have, Caleb.

Cricket song filled the air around her, and an unexpected peace drifted on the wings of their symphony. She might not have the strength of Caleb's faith, but she certainly knew the same God.

"Lord, we need help." Instead of disrupting the melody that surrounded her, her whispered prayer blended in a beautiful harmony. "I've tried everything I know, and it hasn't worked. I'm out of ideas. So if there's something you want me to do, something that will save Brent and Caleb, please tell me." She gulped. "*Guide* me, Lord."

Even the crickets grew quiet in the silence that followed her prayer. Lauren waited, but no angel appeared to show her the way, no flashing arrow illuminated the night sky.

But an idea did occur, so subtle as to be mistaken for her own thought. She didn't feel comfortable contacting the police or the local FBI. No doubt there were hundreds of honest officers in both organizations, but she doubted her ability to find them.

There was one group of officials she trusted, though.

Working quickly, Lauren gathered the weathered wooden slats from the dilapidated bench into a bundle and grabbed the ripped bag of charcoal. When she picked it up, her hopes soared into the sky. Beneath it lay a plastic bottle of lighter fluid.

She shouldered the duffel bag and then placed a call on her cell phone.

"9-1-1 dispatch," the lady on the other line said. "Please state the nature of your emergency."

"Fire," Lauren shouted into the phone. "There's a fire at 5927 Jefferson Avenue. Hurry. There's a baby trapped inside."

She disconnected the call, fighting a flash of guilt at the addition of an imaginary endangered child. The presence of a baby was sure to bring a quick response, and that's what she wanted. That's what Brent and Caleb needed.

Gathering the boards and charcoal in her arms, she dashed around the corner and across the street, toward Caleb's house.

TWENTY-FOUR

"What is taking so long?" Gaines slid his phone open, checked the screen and then shoved it back in the holster clipped to his belt. "How long does it take to make a decision?"

Brent watched him pace to the desk and return. The silent gunmen guarding him and Caleb were obviously nothing more than foot soldiers in Gaines's crooked platoon, but they had both relaxed their postures. The pistol barrel still pointed at Caleb's head, but at least it was no longer pressed against his temple. Brent couldn't get a good look at the guy standing behind him, but he felt the presence of the weapon aimed at the back of his skull like an itch he couldn't scratch.

Caleb had remained almost as quiet as their guards, though he hadn't bothered to hide his silent prayer. Now he entered the conversation.

"So you set Lauren up to take the fall for Frank's murder," he said. "You built a good case against her, and you made sure a whole casino full of witnesses will swear she was with Frank the night he was killed. I get that."

Brent gritted his teeth and worked hard on controlling his fury whenever he glanced at Gaines. That slimy crook. Caleb's tone remained calm, though Brent saw his white-knuckled grip on the chair arms.

Caleb continued. "But how'd you get him to agree to be seen in public with an imposter dressed like her? Seems to me he'd get suspicious of something like that."

"The boss told him that's the way it was gonna be, that's how." Gaines's voice snapped with irritation. "You don't argue with these guys."

"Didn't you just say Frank did?"

"Yeah, and look where it got him."

Jarrell crossed the room and lowered himself onto the couch. His movements were smooth, almost fluid, like a woman's. The jerk even carried a purse, which he tossed onto the cushion. He spared a disdainful glance at Gaines and answered Caleb's question calmly. "Labetti knew Lauren was prepped to take a fall, but he didn't know what kind. He thought we were going to pin her with something to do with the finances, and that night in the casino was nothing more than a practice run. I told him I wanted to be sure I could portray Lauren convincingly in whatever role might come up."

Jarrell's self-control had a slight calming effect on Gaines. When he spoke, some of his growl was gone. "Even after we laid it out, Frank wasn't keen on the idea, but the boss told him if he wanted a personal meeting, he had to cooperate."

Through his anger, Brent saw the logic in their plan. Frank had apparently bought into it, and that's why he'd shipped the money to Lauren's attention instead of his own. If discovered, it would add more fuel to the case against Lauren.

Jarrell crossed one leg over the other and locked his fingers around his knee in a posture Brent had seen Lauren adopt many times. "We selected that blackjack table because it was near the casino entrance, in plain sight of the elevators, where we could be seen as people went up to their rooms for the night." Scorn creased his features. "Of course, he proved himself to be as low class as I expected. He drank so much he couldn't walk straight. We weren't putting on an act when I had to practically carry him up to his room."

Brent almost laughed at the irony of a hired thug calling Frank low class. But he couldn't manage even scornful laughter. The sight of Jarrell sitting there pretending to be Lauren made him sick.

"What about the other guy?" Caleb asked. "David Reynolds. What did he do to tick your bosses off?"

"Not a thing. He gambled moderately, and never more than he could pay. My associates tell me he was cooperative when they came to collect."

At the sight of Jarrell's cold smile, the hair at the back of Brent's neck prickled to attention. This man might adopt gentle gestures, but inside he was nothing but a cold-blooded thug.

"He paid his debts, huh?" Sarcasm gave Brent's voice a sharp edge. "Oh, yeah, I can see why you wanted him dead."

The guard behind him apparently took exception to his tone and shoved the gun barrel into the back of his skull. Gasping against the pain that resulted from the sudden movement, Brent's head was forced forward until his chin rested on his chest.

Jarrell brought a pink polished finger up to tap on his lips. "Hmm. I see your point." A smirk twisted the lips beneath the finger. "Unfortunately, Reynolds was in possession of a dangerous piece of information. He knew our organization had short-listed Lauren for the job at Sterling Foods. He thought our goal was simply cautionary, to protect the database being stored there. But when she was arrested for Frank's murder, he might have decided to make that information public. By eliminating him, we've removed the one possible angle that could be used to prove her innocence."

Gaines barked a brusque laugh. "Yeah, and actually, Reynolds unwittingly helped us come up with a convincible motive to pin the girl with murder. We've made it look like she and Labetti were having a love affair, and it's no secret that she and Reynolds were seeing each other in the past. So we paint her as a crazed, jilted woman who's out to blow away all her exes."

The detective stepped in front of Brent, grabbed his chin between his thumb and forefinger and jerked his head back. He towered over him, glaring.

"It's gonna work out great when we pin her for your murder, too."

The boards in her arms clanked together as Lauren ran, and sounded like cannon shots to her nerve-sensitive ears. All the way across the street, she felt as though she was running in a spotlight. Surely someone would peek through the blinds any minute and see her.

She dashed into the cover of the deep shadow at the side of Caleb's house and skidded to a halt in the sandy soil. Her heart thundered, more from fright than exertion, and she spent a precious few seconds catching her breath and willing her pulse to slow. A peek around the corner showed everything exactly as it had been. As far as she could tell, even the two guys standing outside of the house up the street hadn't noticed her.

The fire department would be here any minute. She had to get a respectable fire going quickly, so they could locate the house by the flames. And it had to be convincing.

Moving as quietly as possible with an arm full of rotting wood planks, she slipped around to the back of the house. A quick glance at the door, and she allowed herself a relieved sigh. The mini-blinds were still closed. At least she wouldn't be seen if someone happened to glance toward the window. They'd have to open the blinds in order to see outside.

She set the wood down in the dirt rather than risk a noise when it hit the cement porch. Then she built a careful pile around the awning post directly in front of the back door. The wooden post was sturdier than the bench planks, but it looked old, with peeling paint and a few splintered places. It *should* catch fire, with a little encouragement.

As she placed the planks around the base of the post, a memory surfaced sharply. Years ago, when she was a young teenager, she and Daddy had spent a week at a ski lodge in Switzerland. Daddy had shown her how to build a fire in the fireplace. The wood had to be arranged precisely in order to ensure an evenly distributed flame. A sloppily laid fire might result in a burning log rolling off and out of the fireplace, and that could burn the house down.

Lauren permitted herself a grim smile. That was the goal.

She laid the planks in a crisscross pattern around the post, then added some of the longer pieces in a tepee shape. A little sand mounded around the base would help keep them in place. Hopefully, when the flame caught, they'd burn all the way up the post.

Now, for the kindling.

She picked up the duffel bag. Beads of sweat broke

out on her forehead. This money belonged to the
Mafia, and she was about to make a bonfire out of it.
But what choice did she have? If she sprayed the wood
with lighter fluid, it would flame for a second, but it
might not catch. She needed something that would burn
quickly but last long enough to allow the fire to do its
work on the wood. According to her father, the trick
to a good fire was the kindling. And in this treeless,
barren yard, she had nothing else available.

With her teeth set together, she started shoving cash
between the boards.

When she was satisfied that her work was as good as
she could make it, she picked up the lighter fluid. Judg-
ing by the weight, it was about half-full. She flipped
the lid open and doused the woodpile, money and the
center post all the way up to the crossbeam to which
the awning was attached. A little fluid remained when
she judged she had enough, so she squirted the rest on
the two outside posts, just for good measure.

A distant sound reached her ears as she snatched the
disposable lighter off the plastic table. A wailing siren.
The fire department was on the way.

She squatted on her haunches and held the lighter
near a couple of one-hundred-dollar bills protruding
from inside the wooden planks, and flicked. Sparks
erupted, but no flame.

*Oh, no! Maybe the boys left this lighter here because
it's empty. God, please, help!*

She held her breath and tried again. A feeble blue
flame flickered to life. Her hand trembled as she held
it at the edge of the money.

Please let this work.

It did. Fire curled the edge of the bills and crept
backward toward the wood.

In an instant, a flash of heat blew Lauren backward and sent her sprawling on her backside in the dirt. She covered her eyes and pressed her singed eyelashes, smelled burning hair and frantically doused a flame in her blond tresses.

When she looked up, her mouth fell open. The fire she'd created was truly awesome. Furious flames licked upward toward the awning inside the porch and leaped into the sky outside. Those wooden planks must have been truly rotten to catch so quickly. And the frame of Caleb's porch wasn't far behind. Already, she could see tongues of fire licking the crossbeam. In a matter of minutes, the entire porch would be engulfed in flame.

Maybe she shouldn't have burned the money after all.

The siren's wail grew louder. Scrambling to her feet, she ran toward the front of the house, confident her fire would draw the attention she wanted.

TWENTY-FIVE

Gaines's cell phone chirped. Brent's pulse pounded loud in his ears and caught Caleb's eye. Was this the call that would end their lives?

Gaines snatched the phone off his belt and slid it open. "Yeah?"

His lips tightened into a white line as he listened. He ducked his head and half turned from the rest of the room, his entire body tense. Brent saw cords standing out in his neck, and a red flush crept across his face. Apparently the detective was receiving a dressing-down from his Cicalo bosses, and he didn't like it one bit. No one in the room spoke, and another sound reached Brent's ears beyond the silence. A siren outside. Sounded pretty close.

Finally, Gaines jerked a single nod. "Understood." He ended the call and faced the room.

Before he could speak, Jarrell sat up straight on the couch. "What is that, an ambulance?"

The detective dismissed his concern with a wave. "It's nothing. We get calls for this lousy neighborhood all night long. Some tweaker probably overdosed on meth." His gaze slid to Caleb. "Maybe even your buddy Mush."

Caleb didn't reply, but his jaw bunched with the effort. Brent listened to the siren growing louder. Hope flickered in the midst of the tension that filled him. Did that siren have anything to do with them?

If he hadn't been watching Caleb's face, he would have missed the sudden widening of his eyes. The big man's gaze fixed on something behind Brent's head for a moment, then slid back to lock onto his face. An unreadable message lay in those eyes. Brent fought an almost irresistible desire to turn his head and see what Caleb had noticed.

"We've been given the go-ahead," Gaines told Jarrell. "You got the weapon?"

Jarrell nodded and grabbed the handbag he'd tossed in the corner of the couch. From it, he pulled a handgun. Brent didn't know much about guns, so he couldn't identify the brand, but one thing was immediately recognizable. The barrel of this pistol was extra long, because of the silencer screwed onto the end.

"Now, here's how it's gonna go." Gaines took a step closer, a twisted smirk on his face.

He's enjoying this, the jerk.

"Mr. Jarrell here is going to shoot both of you. After I make sure you're dead, my associates and I will leave. Five minutes later, Mr. Jarrell will remove the silencer and fire two more shots into your bodies."

Fear throbbed in Brent's chest, and the ache in his ribs intensified. "You're going to shoot us again after we're dead?"

Jarrell snickered. "Don't worry. You won't feel it."

The detective ignored the interruption. "When those shots are heard by neighbors, our fake Lauren Bradley will be seen running through the front door and squealing tires during her escape in a white Grand

Am." Gaines looked at Brent. "Your rental car, which we removed from the Hollywood Casino's parking lot."

"What about the money?"

Jarrell asked the question absently as he rose from the couch and made his way across the room, his gaze fixed on the front window. Outside the sirens had grown much louder. They must have been going somewhere on this street.

Were they coming here?

Brent locked gazes with Caleb. The shadow of a smile played about the corners of the man's lips.

"We'll get it back when we catch up with her. And if a straight cop gets her first, then her possession of the money will serve to further incriminate her. They're willing to let the fifty K go if it makes the case more solid." The sirens were so loud now that even Gaines took notice. His brow creased as he fixed a quizzical look on the closed front door.

The sirens wailed to a stop.

Jarrell lifted a finger and raised one of the mini-blind slats to peek through. Then he jerked around in the room, his eyes round as eight-balls.

When Lauren rounded the house, she saw the flashing red light from an approaching fire truck. An ambulance followed closely behind.

"Here." Her shout didn't carry above the shrieking sirens, but she ran out into the street, waving her arms above her head. "It's here."

Was anyone looking out the window of the house? Probably. Any minute she'd feel a bullet in her back, but she couldn't think about that now. She'd committed herself to this plan, and if it didn't work, they were all going to end up dead anyway.

Lord, please!

The fire truck screeched to a halt in front of her, and the sirens of both vehicles dwindled to silence. She turned to point at the house and experienced a momentary flash of satisfaction. The flames from her fire were clearly visible, leaping into the black sky from the rear of the house.

She had no idea what was happening inside Caleb's home, but she needed to ensure a dramatic entrance.

Half a dozen fully geared firefighters leaped off the engine and took off at a run down the driveway, toward the backyard.

She grabbed a man's strong arm as he dashed by her. "The back of the house is in flames, and I can't get the front door opened. There's a baby!"

Without a moment's hesitation, the man whirled back toward the truck to grab an ax and shouted to his partners. "There's an infant inside. We gotta go through the front."

Two of the men continued down the driveway, but the rest ran to the front door. The firefighter with the ax ran up the walkway in two giant steps, raised his ax and brought it down. The doorknob shattered. The second he stepped back, another firefighter rushed the door and hit a powerful blow with his shoulder.

The door crashed open.

TWENTY-SIX

Jarrell didn't have time to utter a sound. A loud crack filled the house, and in the next second, the door crashed inward. Brent watched as the heavy wood slab swung violently on its hinges and smashed into the impostor. The sound of shattering glass and a moan emitted from behind the door as yellow-clad firefighters rushed into the room.

"What the—"

The goon guarding Caleb didn't finish his sentence. Amazed, Brent watched as the big man sprang into action. In the space of a few seconds, Caleb reached backward, snatched the gun with one hand, and at the same instant hooked his arm around the man's neck. He gave a mighty jerk forward, and the goon sailed over his back and landed with a crash on the floor at his feet. Caleb lurched forward, delivered a stunning blow, then leaped toward the shattered door.

Brent didn't waste time. Instinct took over. He sprang up from his chair, at the same time twisting his body around backward toward the man behind him. Pain exploded in his injured ribs and snatched his breath, but he didn't spend time thinking about that. As he twisted, he locked his arm and delivered a blow to the gunman's hand with his elbow. The gun went off as it skittered across the carpeted floor, and his ears rang in the aftermath of the blast. Acting on instinct, the man shot a terrified glance toward the firefighters and his buddy on the floor, and whirled. Brent was after him in a minute and caught up within two steps. He extended his hands and used the force of his body to shove the guy hard into the wall. His head hit with a painful-sounding thud. Stunned, the man bounced back into Brent's waiting arms.

"What is going on here?" The firefighter's angry bellow echoed nearly as loudly as the gunfire. "Where's the baby?"

The question served to still all action in the room for a second. Brent and the man he now held by an arm twisted behind his back—a move he learned from watching cop shows on television—both turned to face him. Caleb emerged from behind the abused front door, Boyd Jarrell's pistol in one hand and his other arm hooked around Jarrell's throat. Jarrell's face was an ugly shade of purple, and his eyes were beginning to bulge.

Gaines recovered his tongue. "Good work, men. You've arrived just in time to help us apprehend these criminals and take them into custody." He slid a badge case out of his pocket and flipped it open.

"He's lying." Brent shoved the man he held into the room. "We're not the criminals, they are. They were getting ready to kill us."

The firefighter inspected the detective's badge, distrust still etched in deep lines across his forehead.

Gaines awarded Brent a nasty smile. "Nice try, but these men aren't going to be taken in by your lies." He turned to the firefighter. "Call the Las Vegas police to verify. I'll give you the direct number to my division. They know all about tonight's bust."

"Don't do it, man. These slime buckets are on the Cicalo payroll. They're either going to put you in touch with another crooked cop, or directly with their Mafia boss."

Caleb's deep voice resonated with composure, though how he managed it Brent didn't know. His heart was pumping adrenaline through his veins with the force of water through a fire hose.

That the firefighters had heard of the Cicalo gang was obvious by the apprehensive look that dawned on their faces.

"Again, nice try." Gaines adopted a superior sneer. "It's *these* men who are on the Cicalo payroll."

One of the firefighters standing just inside the doorway spoke to the one who was obviously in charge. "I don't know, Tony. Maybe we ought to call 9-1-1."

At that moment, a figure slid around him in the doorway and entered the room.

Lauren!

A wave of relief rocked Brent to the core. He drank in the sight of her like a dying man savoring the water of life. Her clothes were dingy with dirt, her hair disheveled, black streaks smudged one side of her face, and she was still the most beautiful woman he had ever seen. He couldn't tear his gaze away from her. When she caught sight of him, the smile that leaped onto her face shone like a beacon that could light the darkest night.

Then she turned an imploring look up to Tony. "Please don't do that. I'm very sorry I lied about the baby. I wanted to make sure you took these men by surprise. My friends are telling the truth. These people are members of the Mafia, and they're trying to frame me for murdering two men. That's why I called you instead of 9-1-1. We don't know who in the police department might be involved."

Tony didn't appear convinced by her plea. Furrows gouged his brow as he studied her.

Then he caught sight of Jarrell.

Brent watched as he registered the similarity between the two. The man's eyes moved as his gaze bounced back and forth between them. Then Caleb, with a smile, placed a ham-size hand on the top of Jarrell's head and ripped the blond wig off.

Tony's mouth dropped open.

Lauren pulled a cell phone from her pocket and offered it to him. "I recommend the FBI. There's a man named Agent Lawson in Washington D.C. who is probably expecting a call. The national hotline number is on my call log."

Brent wanted to laugh out loud. *Good girl!*

Apparently Detective Gaines didn't plan to wait around for the FBI. Moving with surprising speed, he made a dash toward the kitchen, away from Tony and his team. The firefighters couldn't move as quickly, weighed down as they were by their heavy gear and equipment.

Brent shoved the man he held toward the nearest obstacle, the chair in which he'd been sitting. He had time to see the guy fall forward over the chair back before he dashed after Gaines, but he wasn't quick enough. The detective reached the back door before he could stop him.

When the door opened, he was met with a wall of fire.

* * *

Lauren sat on the couch between Brent and Caleb, watching as federal agents handcuffed Gaines, Jarrell and the two crooked cops. Feds swarmed over the house and yard, and blue lights flashed in an almost peaceful rhythm through the open front door.

A clean-cut man wearing a crisp white shirt and slacks detached himself from Tony and another pair of firefighters in the kitchen, and came to stand before them.

"Everybody here okay?" he asked.

Beside her Brent winced and fingered the bandage around his abdomen with a ginger touch. The paramedics had said he had a broken rib and needed to go to the hospital for an X-ray to make sure that was the only damage. They were waiting until the FBI released them.

"Yeah, we're okay." His brave smile looked a little pasted on from this angle.

"Good. We're going to get you an escort to the hospital to get those ribs checked out, then they'll bring you downtown to join your friends. We've got a long list of questions we need to get through."

Lauren edged a touch closer to Brent. When she'd seen Gaines and Jarrell enter Caleb's house, she'd feared she would never see Brent alive again. Thank goodness she'd been wrong. Now she didn't ever want to leave his side.

"Can't I go with him?" she asked.

The man considered for a moment. "I don't see why not." He jerked his head toward Gaines and the others, who were being led through the front door. "Processing those four will take a while anyway."

"What's going to happen to them?" Caleb asked.

The federal agent shook his head. "That's not for me to say, but I sure wouldn't want to be in their shoes. Jarrell is staying closemouthed, but Gaines has already started to sing. Even gave us the name of his Cicalo contacts. Apparently the guy thinks he can cut a deal, but there's no way he's going to avoid prison time over this." An ominous shadow darkened his features as he stared after the detective. "I'm afraid he'll discover there are almost as many loyal Cicalo employees on the inside as out."

Lauren didn't bother to suppress a shudder at the thought of the detective's fate in prison.

The agent looked back at her. "He said something about some missing money."

"Oh, I forgot." She gave an embarrassed laugh. "There's a little left. It's in a duffel bag in the backyard. I'm afraid I used the rest as kindling."

Brent's jaw dropped open. "You burned fifty thousand dollars?"

"Not all of it," Lauren told him with an innocent smile. "I kept a couple of bundles in case it needed to be used as evidence or something."

Caleb's deep, rumbling laughter filled the room.

"Thanks for leaving us something to go on." The agent's tone was so dry a match might have ignited it.

"Here's something else to go on." Brent lifted an arm, his movements cautious, and pointed at the desk in the corner. "On that computer you'll find more data about the Cicalos' online gambling ring than you know what to do with. Hundreds of thousands of bets totaling millions of dollars. The data is encrypted, but I saved the code on the hard drive where your tech folks can find it easily."

A smile spread across the agent's face. "This is exactly the break we've been looking for. The folks in the organized-crime unit are going to do backflips over this." He instructed one of the other agents to secure the computer, then turned back to Brent. "Let me go see if the paramedics are ready for you yet."

He disappeared in the direction of the front yard.

Caleb leaned forward and peered at her, his eyes narrow. "You set my house on fire, sister."

The mock anger in his voice failed to chastise her, because she saw a smile tugging at the corners of his mouth.

"Only your porch," she replied. "And only to save your life."

"What made you decide to set a fire?" Brent asked. "Why did you think you could trust the Las Vegas Fire Department?"

Lauren looked at her hands in her lap. She couldn't explain why. There had been no angelic appearance, no flashing arrows pointing the way. But the decision had felt right.

She shrugged her shoulders, feeling a little shame-faced because of her earlier outburst. "I prayed for guidance," she said simply. "I think God answered."

Caleb placed a strong arm around her shoulders and gave her a gentle squeeze. "Well done, sister. Well done." He slapped his hands on his thighs and heaved to his feet. "If I'm going to be spending time downtown answering questions, I'd better see about securing that broken door. Otherwise my good neighbors will clean me out."

He strode after the FBI agent, leaving them alone.

Lauren turned on the cushion. She searched Brent's face, drinking in his features like a thirsty sponge soaks up water. Tiny lines creased the skin on either side of his mouth. He shifted his weight, and when the movement caused him pain, the creases deepened. Her heart twisted with sympathy.

"Are you okay?" She gestured toward his bandage.

"I'm fine, thanks to you." His hand rose, and he grasped a lock of her hair. "You burned your hair."

"It'll grow back." She was incapable of tearing her gaze from his. "I thought I would never see you again."

His fingers released her hair, but he didn't lower his hand. Instead, warm fingers brushed her cheek. "Did the idea bother you?"

The strength of their locked gazes intensified. Wordlessly, she nodded.

"I thought I'd lost you, too." His whisper fell like a feather between them. "I don't ever want to lose you, Lauren."

His eyes drew her closer. When his fingers slipped around to the back of her neck, she felt a gentle pressure as he pulled her forward. An intense joy flooded her heart, while her insides vibrated with the meaning of his words.

He loves me, too!

"You won't ever lose me." Her promise caressed his soft lips in the moment before they touched hers.

EPILOGUE

"**I** can't believe this is the way we're spending the night before your wedding." Mason pulled a picture off the wall of Brent's tiny living room and added it to a big box near Caleb's feet. He leveled a disgusted glare at Brent. "Most guys go out and party the night before they click the lock on the old ball and chain." He blanched as he realized what he'd said. His gaze shifted to Lauren. "No offense intended."

"No offense taken," Lauren assured him. She'd long ago forgiven Mason for suspecting her of being a black widow. He'd had plenty of reason, after all. The Cicalo gang had done their job well and almost got away with it.

"I'm not interested in what most guys do." Brent's arm slipped around her and pulled her to his side. "Tomorrow, after this woman has my ring on her finger, that's when I'll party."

Laughing, she dropped the piece of newspaper she'd been ready to wrap around a dish and nestled close to him. "You two have no idea what you're in for," she told his friends. "My father and stepmother have gone all out for the reception."

Brent nodded. "Lawrence Bradley doesn't do anything halfway, especially when it's for his only daughter."

Lauren's mind ticked over tomorrow's elaborate arrangements. It really might be an embarrassment of extravagance. Hiring the famous chef Ambrose to cater a formal dinner for three hundred people was expensive enough, but the list of well-known entertainers scheduled to perform after dinner was just plain mortifying. Even Brent had no concept of the extent Daddy had gone to to make sure his daughter's wedding was an event on the scale of a celebrity's.

Caleb finished unscrewing a shelf on the entertainment center and leaned it against the wall. "All I can say, sister, is there better be some good food if I have to wear a monkey suit to get it."

She laughed at the big man. "Don't worry. The food will be great."

"I can't tell you how much we appreciate you coming all the way out here for the wedding," Brent told him.

Caleb set the screwdriver down and crossed the room in two strides. He plunged his hand into the bowl of popcorn on the coffee table and sank into a sitting position on the floor.

"I wouldn't miss it," he told Brent. "I've been looking forward to this day for nine months, from the minute I first laid eyes on you two. Of course, I didn't know you were going to put me to work packing and moving you when I got here." He tossed a handful of white puffy kernels in his mouth.

A short break sounded good. Lauren tugged Brent toward the couch and then settled in beside him. "If Brent weren't so busy at work, he would have gotten his stuff packed up long before now."

"Can't be helped." He leaned forward and grabbed

his soda can from the table. "My team's been working overtime to implement a new security system for the Sterling Foods computer network. It just went live a couple of days ago."

"Just in time to free Brent up for our honeymoon." She smiled at him.

Her job had kept her busy lately, too. She'd only been with her new company for four months, but Becky, her new boss, had proved more than understanding about the upcoming wedding and honeymoon trip.

Mason sealed the flaps on the box at his feet, then sank to the floor beside Caleb. "Just so everyone knows, I'm still bitter about missing all the action in Vegas. Next time you discover an illegal Mafia gambling operation, give me enough notice to fly out there, okay?"

Brent and Caleb laughed, but the idea of any further connection with the Mafia sent a shudder rippling through Lauren's body.

Brent took a gulp from his can. "You might not have been there, but we couldn't have done it without you, buddy."

"That's right. We made a good team." Caleb gave a satisfied nod. "We nailed a bad cop, exposed a dangerous impostor and cleared Lauren's name. It took all of us to do that."

Brent's arm tightened around her. "That's right."

Mason's hand, loaded with popcorn, stopped halfway to his mouth. "You know what? You're right. We do make a good team."

His thoughtful tone drew their attention.

Caleb eyed him, brows low over his eyes. "Yeah, so?"

"So, why break up a good thing?" Mason spoke

slowly, putting the words together as he fleshed out his idea. "You have no idea how often innocent people are falsely accused of a crime." His gaze slid to Lauren. "Not all of them are as lucky as you."

The back of Lauren's neck prickled as she glimpsed where Mason was heading. "Go on," she said.

"So, why don't we do something about it?" The flow of his words gained speed as his excitement grew. "We could work together to help people who are falsely accused." He looked at Brent. "You've got the technical skills to help us crack codes and hack systems, and find anything we need on the computer. And I can ferret out all kinds of information. Plus, I know all the tricks an investigator needs to know."

That was true. Brent had told Lauren about Mason's background, how he used to be a law-enforcement officer back in New Mexico, but quit the job and moved here to Atlanta when his wife was murdered.

"What about me? What's my role?" Caleb glared sideways at Mason. "And if you say I'm the muscle-bound thug who keeps the bad guys in line, I'll smack you upside the head."

"You could be the spiritual adviser." Lauren was only half teasing. Caleb's strong faith and wisdom had certainly taught her how to listen to God's guiding nudges.

She felt Brent's muscles tense. Mason's excitement was contagious, and Brent had caught it. He leaned forward and pointed a finger in Caleb's direction.

"No, you're the contact guy. The people you see every day know things we have no access to."

"But they're all out in Vegas."

"Not true," Mason said. "You lived in Atlanta all your life. You've been working with scum for years, first as a jailer here, and then as…" His hand waved vaguely and dismissively in the air. "As whatever it is you do now. Surely you picked up some contacts along the way."

Caleb's fingers stroked his jaw with slow, thoughtful movement. "I do have a few contacts among the lawless and less fortunate, now that you mention it. And I've been thinking about coming home to Atlanta. My mother isn't getting any younger, and I'd like to be close by in case she needs me."

"There you go." Mason jumped to his feet, unable to stay still another minute. "We can call ourselves the Falsely Accused Support Team. FAST for short."

Brent pulled away slightly so he could look into her face. Questions hovered in his eyes and, behind them, the flicker of enthusiasm for Mason's idea. "What do you think, baby?"

Pleasure washed over her. He was asking her opinion before he committed. If she said no, she knew without a doubt that he wouldn't do it. He'd walk away from something he wanted to do, just because she didn't want him to.

Oh, Lord, how did I ever manage to find someone like him?

She knew the answer before the question had finished forming in her mind. She hadn't found him. God had, and He'd guided Brent to trust her when she most needed help.

"I think it's a terrific idea," she said.

She saw her own smile reflected in her fiancé's eyes in the moment before he swept her into a kiss.

* * * * *

Dear Reader,

One of the best parts of being a writer is doing the research. Of course, I love setting my books in fun places, because then I have an excuse for visiting! Even though I'm not a gambler, Las Vegas is an inspiring city full of incredible sights and experiences. I had to rein myself in when I wrote *Dangerous Impostor*, because I wanted to describe them all, even the places that didn't have a part in the story.

Celebrity impersonators are fascinating people, and Vegas is full of them. Elvis, of course, is everywhere. When I first got the idea for this book, it was going to be about an Elvis impersonator. I had a great time posing for pictures with old Elvis and young Elvis, with slim Elvis and puffy Elvis. That story didn't work out, but the idea of impersonators grew until I'd built an entire Las Vegas Casino around the theme. The Hollywood Hotel and Casino is totally fictitious, but I think it's a terrific idea, don't you?

I hope you've enjoyed this story, and the sights and sounds of Las Vegas, Nevada. I'd love to know what you think! Contact me through www.VirginiaSmith.org, or become my friend on Facebook at http://www.facebook.com/ginny.p.smith. Or you can write to me: Virginia Smith, P.O. Box 70271, West Valley City, Utah 84170.

Virginia Smith

Questions for Discussion

1. Have you ever been accused of something you didn't do? If so, how were your feelings similar to Lauren's? How were they different?

2. When Lauren begins to feel an attraction to Brent, she refuses to let herself give in to her feelings because of her past relationship with her former boss. Are office romances ever appropriate? What are the risks involved?

3. Lauren is also reluctant to rely on Brent to help her out of trouble. Why?

4. Several celebrity impersonators make an appearance in *Dangerous Impostor*. Which one would you like to meet in person?

5. As evidence against Lauren stacks up, Brent is increasingly suspicious, but he persists in believing her. Why? Have you ever chosen to trust your instincts rather than facts?

6. Who did you suspect of killing Frank, and why?

7. In order to avoid drawing notice, Brent tells Lauren several times, "Just act like you belong." Does that work in real life?

8. Lauren has always operated under the premise that "The Lord helps those who help themselves." Brent believes that the Lord sends help when we

need it. Do you think either of these opinions is better than the other?

9. Lauren is not entirely comfortable with the neighborhood Caleb lives in or with the people he welcomes into his home. Why? Is there any evidence that she changes her opinion?

10. Which character did you find most appealing?

INSPIRATIONAL

Wholesome romances that touch the heart and soul.

celebrating 15 YEARS

COMING NEXT MONTH
AVAILABLE MARCH 13, 2012

EYE OF THE STORM
Hannah Alexander

THE DETECTIVE'S SECRET DAUGHTER
Fitzgerald Bay
Rachelle McCalla

BROKEN TRUST
Sharon Dunn

SHADES OF TRUTH
Undercover Cops
Sandra Orchard

LISCNM0212

REQUEST YOUR FREE BOOKS!

2 FREE RIVETING INSPIRATIONAL NOVELS
PLUS 2 FREE MYSTERY GIFTS

YES! Please send me 2 FREE Love Inspired® Suspense novels and my 2 FREE mystery gifts (gifts are worth about $10). After receiving them, if I don't wish to receive any more books, I can return the shipping statement marked "cancel". If I don't cancel, I will receive 4 brand-new novels every month and be billed just $4.49 per book in the U.S. or $4.99 per book in Canada. That's a saving of at least 22% off the cover price. It's quite a bargain! Shipping and handling is just 50¢ per book in the U.S. and 75¢ per book in Canada.* I understand that accepting the 2 free books and gifts places me under no obligation to buy anything. I can always return a shipment and cancel at any time. Even if I never buy another book, the two free books and gifts are mine to keep forever.

123/323 IDN FEHR

Name   (PLEASE PRINT)

Address   Apt. #

City   State/Prov.   Zip/Postal Code

Signature (if under 18, a parent or guardian must sign)

Mail to the **Reader Service:**
IN U.S.A.: P.O. Box 1867, Buffalo, NY 14240-1867
IN CANADA: P.O. Box 609, Fort Erie, Ontario L2A 5X3

Not valid for current subscribers to Love Inspired Suspense books.

Are you a subscriber to Love Inspired Suspense
and want to receive the larger-print edition?
Call 1-800-873-8635 or visit www.ReaderService.com.

* Terms and prices subject to change without notice. Prices do not include applicable taxes. Sales tax applicable in N.Y. Canadian residents will be charged applicable taxes. Offer not valid in Quebec. This offer is limited to one order per household. All orders subject to credit approval. Credit or debit balances in a customer's account(s) may be offset by any other outstanding balance owed by or to the customer. Please allow 4 to 6 weeks for delivery. Offer available while quantities last.

Your Privacy—The Reader Service is committed to protecting your privacy. Our Privacy Policy is available online at www.ReaderService.com or upon request from the Reader Service.

We make a portion of our mailing list available to reputable third parties that offer products we believe may interest you. If you prefer that we not exchange your name with third parties, or if you wish to clarify or modify your communication preferences, please visit us at www.ReaderService.com/consumerschoice or write to us at Reader Service Preference Service, P.O. Box 9062, Buffalo, NY 14269. Include your complete name and address.

LISUS11B